The Priestess & The Trow

The Seventh Tale from the Dragonsbane Inn

By

Adam Berk

Adam Berk

The Priestess & The Trow

The Seventh Tale from the Dragonsbane Inn

Adam Berk

Copyright © 2023 Adam Berk

All rights reserved.

This book is a work of fiction. Names, characters, places and incidents are either a product of the author's imagination or used fictionally. Any resemblance to actual events, locals, or persons living or dead is entirely coincidental.

ISBN: 9798389213562

Cover Art by Jeff Ward

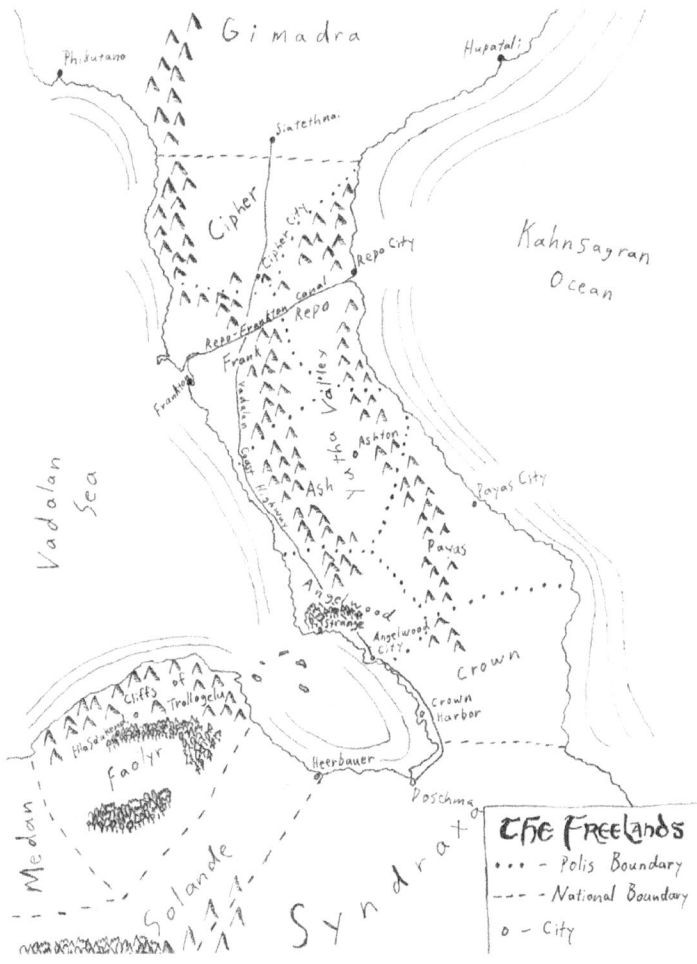

Note: Resemblance between the Freelands of Ardyn and other fantasy lands may not be entirely coincidental.

To my sister, Elise, who taught me the difference between cool and lame—an important and underrated distinction in any civilization.

Books by Adam Berk

The Centaur & The Sot

The Trouble with Trolls

The Swap

On The Wings of Draklings

Mistress of The Golden Cords

Charms

The Priestess and The Trow

Sunderfest (forthcoming)

~ I ~

Ten drams past eight. She's late. That's okay. More time to clean.

Trina finished sweeping the floor of her flat as best she could, jamming her disintegrating broom into the cracks between scuffed cedar planks, and flipping the grit out the front door. She had a good feeling about this. When she'd first moved into the place, she'd vowed never to have another flatmate again, but this felt different.

Gods, I hope she likes living here!

Jeydah Carver had only seen the barmaid's little domicile once before. They'd set up her sleeping palate, vanity, and screens by the hearth making an impromptu bedchamber/kitchen, where once there'd been naught but terra cotta tile separating the hearth from the living room. When Trina'd asked her new flatmate if there was enough space, the elf had looked around, raised her arched eyebrows, tucked a lock of black hair behind a pointed ear and sighed dramatically.

"Reminds me of an assignment I had in a Durvingari mine," she said. "If I can spend two weeks squatting in a dwarvish dump chamber, I can do this."

Vintage Jeydah!

The Trow Elf was the most amazing person Trina'd ever

known and far more interesting than her fellow barmaids at the Dragonsbane Inn. Most were nice enough but only ever interested in drinking and carousing after their shifts or hustling up connections for their burgeoning acting, dancing, or minstreling careers. Jeydah was also more pragmatic than Trina's Demian sisters at the Temple of the Cavorting Incarnate. Those vixes couldn't talk about the weather without turning it into a discourse on raising prajja energy and power centers. From the moment they'd met, the barmaid had felt she and the elf should be friends.

That moment had been eight moons ago, when she and her paramour, the master barkeep Garret Stockwell, had gone drakling riding with Jeydah and the apprentice barkeep, Farian Daringsford. Things had taken a horrific turn when Trina'd been taken hostage by a Syndraxan spy, but the Trow Elf and the master barkeep had literally flown to her rescue and chased the spy down on dragonback. Afterward, Jeydah had revealed her connection to the Gardeners, an international network of assassins.

They didn't see each other again for nearly eight months after that. Farian would flob about with Jeydah from time to time, but Garret wanted nothing more to do with her. Angelwood was dangerous enough, he said, without associating with professional killers. Nevertheless, Trina had thought of the feisty little trow often, remembering woman's strength and wit as she spoke of her travels and intrigues.

Then one day, while Trina was window-shopping her way down Hillrise Avenue, she saw Jeydah in the street in front of an abandoned building. The elf was hopping mad, cursing loudly as she kicked the locked door and punched the boarded-up windows. Other pedestrians, no strangers to strangeness in the bustling Freelandish polis, continued their conversations and errands while crossing to the other side of the road.

But Trina had no problem talking to crazy folk. On the contrary, in her experience they were usually safer and more honest than so-called "normal" people. So she approached the unhinged elf with her winningest smile.

The Priestess & The Trow

"Need some help?"

The offer took Jeydah by surprise. Her arching brows pinched in confusion as she turned. Then she saw the barmaid and her full lips twisted in a wry grimace.

"No, Trina. Just having a little disagreement with my employers. *I* think I need a store to run and a place to live while I'm on probation. *They* apparently think otherwise, the blighted, rot-pocking, kull-snarfing, shest-eaters!"

She punctuated the last with a thrust kick that cracked one of the boards on the former store's window. Trina looked the building over. She remembered Jeydah talking about her woodworking shop. She'd been quite proud of it even though the Gardeners maintained it as a front for their operations.

"Wow, they really shut your place down, didn't they? It looks like it's been abandoned for years!"

"That's how they do things."

Jeydah heaved a sigh, slouching against the chained and padlocked door.

"Froze my expense account, too. I have another week until rent's due and then—"

She threw up her arms as though trying to fling her troubles into the air like chaff. Trina winced. She'd been homeless before. It wasn't something she'd wish on anyone.

"Do you have somewhere to go? You could stay at my place if you need to."

Jeydah was reluctant, but they talked it over anyway at a Medanite bistro across the road from the White Mountain Playhouse. They had cocktails along with a light meal of bread and sautéed valley quail seasoned with ground nuts, olive oil, and herbs. After the third round of sparkling white wine and fefoni sours the suspended assassin finally swallowed her pride and accepted Trina's offer.

Now, a week later, as the setting sun made the walls blush orange and amber, the barmaid was about to finish her day of cleaning by sweeping the front landing, when the bell at her building's front gate rang. She rushed down the stairs and across the courtyard to find Jeydah standing there.

Adam Berk

The elf looked uncharacteristically contrite, her small shoulders slumped, her long, black hair falling forward so it nearly obscured her dark, clever eyes and wide, smirking smile. There was a trunk at her side and what appeared to be an enormous white fluffy boa with orange splotches draped over her shoulders. Suddenly, the boa raised its head and stretched a pair of soft-feathered wings behind Jeydah's head. Trina saw then it was actually the Trow Elf's pet.

"Sorry I'm late," she said. "Rhys got into the pantry cupboard and wouldn't come out."

"Aw," said Trina as she opened the gate. "Is the move upsetting him?"

"Yes, he doesn't like new things. Until he gets used to your place, he's going to be a very grumpy miffin, isn't he? Yes he is."

Jeydah rubbed two fingers on the side of the creature's feathery face. It endured the attention a moment, its wide eyes half-lidded in annoyance before turning its head disdainfully away.

"He's cute." Trina regarded the creature with apprehension.

Jeydah had told the barmaid about her pet during their lunch together. Rhys was a miffin, or miniature griffin, bred down by the beast dealers at Gripper's Stables. He had an owl's head and talons with fluffy white feathers that blended with downy fur on his feline hindquarters—white except for orange splotches on his back, tail, and plumicorns.

Trina, who hadn't had a pet since a spaniel pup her parents let her keep as a child, was at a loss. Should she treat it like a cat or a bird? She offered a finger by way of introduction, then quickly snapped it back as the miffin tried to bite it with its little pink beak.

"Rhys!" Jeydah exclaimed. "You be nice! Sorry about that. I'm sure he'll settle down once we get inside."

This was not the case.

As soon as the two of them hauled the Trow Elf's trunk up the stairs, into the flat and over to her sleeping palate, the

The Priestess & The Trow

creature let out a screech and launched itself at Trina's head. The barmaid ducked with a yelp as the excited miffin flew past, then tore about the chamber in frantic circles. He knocked over her standing cloak rack, scrabbled over her dinner table, talons digging gouges in the maple wood surface, and finally perched atop her bookcase where he glared down at both of them ruefully.

"Blood and iron!" Jeydah exclaimed, walking over to the bookcase, standing on tiptoe, and reaching up to the creature. "I've never seen him so worked up! I'm sure it's just the excitement of being in a new place."

Or he hates me.

Rhys rubbed his face on his mistress' extended fingers, glaring at Trina as though confirming her suspicion.

"Sorry about this. Lucky you don't seem to have anything too valuable around."

"The bookcase is desert oak," Trina grated, the sound of the miffin's talons on the wood setting her teeth on edge. "It cost me a month's wages."

"Oh."

Jeydah looked surprised as she appraised the bookcase as though seeing it for the first time.

"So it is. And you *bought* it? I would've thought a girl with your looks would be more interested in—well, no matter. Come on, Rhys. Get off of there. We'll have to get some sort of mat for up here so you can—oh!"

The miffin launched himself over the elf's head and straight into the planter by Trina's window. It wasn't a proper planter, but rather an old feed trough the barmaid had salvaged to grow fresh herbs in. The miffin dug up a thyme plant with his fore-claws, kicked potting soil onto the floor with his hind legs, and pecked at a basil plant, worrying its leaves as though they were the flesh of his prey.

"Rhys, no!" cried Jeydah as she snatched the creature out of the planter. "That was *so* bad! What a bad miffin you are. Oh! So squishy, though. Squish, squish. Yes, so amazingly, wonderfully *squishy!*"

Adam Berk

Trina stared as the elf smooshed the fluffy, feathery bundle to her chest. The creature stared back at her with an ominous glower. There was a great difference, she realized between merely befriending a person and cohabitating with her and her miffin.

Sometime later, the barmaid sat by the window, studying her Demian wantcraft while her new flatmate cursed and clattered about in the background. Jeydah'd insisted on cleaning the flat herself, even though Trina'd spent most of the day doing just that. The elf claimed that though the place *looked* clean, her irritated sinuses bespoke overlooked nooks and crannies doubtless "dirtier than a gnome's nutsack."

"Don't Trow Elves spend all their time outdoors communing with nature and talking to animals?" Trina'd asked.

"Ha!" came the strident reply. "Only because so many human governments won't let us buy property. Just because I know how to work with nature, doesn't mean I like it. Mother Nature's a filthy bitch. I'll take modern comforts over squatting in the dirt any day."

Sometime later, the elf scraped away at the soot built up inside the hearth's smoke shelf with a spatula, griping loudly about the barmaid's lack of cleaning implements. Trina tried to focus on her studies. She'd offered to help with the cleaning, but Jeydah'd waved her away claiming only an elf could know elvish standards—even though Trina'd waited on a fair share of her folk at the inn.

Taking a deep breath to still the irritated tremors rising in her chest, she opened the slim hard cover of *Threading the Wheel: A Beginner's Guide to Practical Wantcraft* and began practicing her rhupas—the combinations of expressions and gestures used by Demian priestesses to connect with the desires of others. She started with her face, focusing on specific thoughts and feelings to bring out a myriad of expressions, each designed to link with a certain energy center in a hypothetical target.

These she checked using her second most prized possession after the bookcase: a full-length mirror. Though its

The Priestess & The Trow

glass was smoky and tinted green, its pewter frame burnished and dented, the device was the most important tool of her craft. Between it, her comfortable chair, her books, and her window, that corner of the room had become her special little sanctuary.

Trina had many interests, but she found the Demian art of coercion profoundly satisfying. It was like learning to fly with wings she'd spent most of her life never knowing she had. Before long, she was immersed in her studies. She rose from her chair to practice her enthralling looks, words, and gestures, then lowered herself back down again to read some more until window darkened, and she was forced to light her meager collection of oil lamps.

By this time, Jeydah had finally cleaned the place to her satisfaction, and the two of them set about preparing the leather fish and vegetables Trina'd bought at the market that morning. The familiar tasks of tending the hearth fire, seasoning the food, and adjusting the heights of the pothooks and skillet rack, did much to ease the irritable tension between the two. By the time they settled down to opposite sides of the dinner table, the irascible elf's smirking smile had returned along with the barmaid's hopes of friendship.

"Sorry about all the cursing," said Jeydah. "I get aggressive when I clean. And that old scrub brush of yours is about as effective as a squashed hedgehog."

"Well, now that half my tips aren't going into the landlord's purse, I'll be sure to get some better cleaning supplies."

Jeydah took a bite of leather fish and looked around with a sigh, her dark eyes wide and hopeful, yet ringed with fatigue.

"Yes," she said, waving her fork as she spoke like a dualist with a poniard. "Yes, I think this could work. It's a small place, but it has everything we need until my trollshest with the Gardeners runs its course. You think it'd be all right if I do some woodworking in the courtyard now and then?"

Trina thought of how she never read books in the courtyard after a lecherous neighbor had tried to chat her up.

Adam Berk

The conversation had ended with him asking if she tasted as good as she looked and licking her face. The barmaid considered how the elvish assassin would respond to such a cad and grinned.

"I think that's a wonderful idea."

"Maybe I can make some baubles to sell on a street corner. Or get a booth on Goddess Pier, or the Veneria Beach boardwalk. You think I can make enough at this barmaid job to cover starting expenses?"

She shot Trina a questioning look, to which the barmaid responded with a sigh and a shrug. Trina had recommended her to work at the Dragonsbane Inn as they were starting to hire new staff for the upcoming Sunderfest holiday season. As the inn was the sort of place where the pretty faces drew more custom than quality service, Jeydah was hired on the spot, despite her lack of experience.

"I wouldn't expect much at first," said the barmaid. "Juggling all those orders in your head takes a while to get the hang of. I'd probably be out on the street by now if I hadn't learned a few tricks for charming guests out of their money."

"Yes, I saw you practicing those in the mirror. Demian wantcraft, right?"

Trina blushed a little as she nodded, falling unconsciously into the rhupa, *you-found-my-secret-sweet*.

"I've nearly completed my six moons as an aspirant, yes."

"Huh. That figures," said Jeydah with a smirk and a sniff.

"Ex*cuse* me?"

"I mean it suits you, that's all. The Cult of the Goddess Demia's all about charming people into doing stuff for you. And, from what you've told me, you do tend to let other people come to your rescue and fight your battles for you."

Trina nearly choked on the bite of sun peas and potato in her mouth. *That's not fair,* she thought as Jeydah's assessment of her sunk in. *In fact, that's almost—no, it* is *the most offensive thing I've ever heard!*

"First of all," said the barmaid, grateful for the controlled breathing exercises she'd learned to keep her voice steady.

The Priestess & The Trow

"Demianism is more than just 'charming people into doing stuff'. It's about connecting with the deeper consciousness of all things."

Jeydah rolled her eyes, and mimicked a man stroking his stalk with her right hand.

"Second," Trina grated. "I don't need others to fight my battles for me!"

"Oh, so when we went Drakling riding last spring, you fought off that Syndraxan spy all by yourself?"

"That's absurd! It's not like I planned to get—"

"And that business with your uncle? When all your friends put their lives at risk breaking into his fairy grove?"

"That was *their* idea!"

"Riiight. I'm sure you batting your beautiful twinkly blues and tossing your golden locks had nothing to do with their decision."

Trina slammed her fork down and rose from the table, her appetite gone.

"If you're implying I used wantcraft on my friends, you couldn't be more wrong! I would *never*—"

"You use wantcraft all the time whether you realize it or not!"

Jeydah rose from the table as well, her voice rising with her. She cleared their plates reflexively as she railed, jerking them off the table in quick angry bursts and flinging them into the washbasin.

"Flirting, cajoling," the elf continued. "Call it what you will, it's still just wiggling your girly bits to get people to do things."

"Yeah? And what do you do? Call it what you will, it's just killing people you don't like for money!"

"Oh-ho! That's not even close! The Gardeners have a strict set of standards for making kills. We only take lives that make the world worse by their *calsahns*—their lives' trajectories."

"Ha! Are your masters gods? I've read enough history to know how random the effects of a person's actions can be on the world. How do you know your masters aren't just selling your services to the highest bidders and making stuff up about your targets 'trajectories' after taking the jobs?"

"What would you know about—?"

Jeydah started to retort, then snapped her mouth shut as though taken aback by the barmaid's solid argument. It surprised Trina as well. She was not used to someone poking so many of her dreamstones at once. And there was something in the condescending way the elf looked at her that made Trina want to hurl the nearest heavy object at her pointy-eared head.

Now, however, her new roommate was giving her an evaluating look, as though truly seeing her for the first time. Perhaps, Trina thought hopefully, she's regretting some of those insulting things she said and is ready to apologize.

"One could *also* ask," Jeydah replied instead, her lips spreading into the wickedest of smiles. "If all your temple's talk of uniting consciousness and threading energy wheels, isn't just propaganda for turning you lot into a bunch of docile little whores."

"Ugh!"

Trina nearly spat. The words hit her like a slap in the face. Too angry to retort, she spun on her heel, stormed into her bedroom and slammed the door.

"That's right," the elf's voice came muffled through the closed door at the barmaid's back. "Run along like a good little lady and leave the cleaning up for someone else!"

I'll clean when you pay rent, you obnoxious, little vagrant! Trina fumed.

But she kept the words to herself. Fighting with Jeydah was becoming the most exhausting part of a long day, and all she wanted to do was wash the night's drama off her face and go to bed. So, she sat at her vanity, filled her wash basin from the bedside pitcher and blotted her face with a cool, wet cloth until her flushed angry features settled into smooth serenity.

Maybe she *was* running away from a fight again, she reflected, but at least she could look good doing it!

~ II ~

Oak and Elder, has my calsahn really come to this?
"So, when guests come in, I like to pretend they're a famous Pit fighter or siren singer, even if they're not. That way they feel extra super-duper special when we serve them!"

Jeydah forced a smile and nodded as though everything the maître d' was telling her *wasn't* the most ridiculous thing she'd ever heard. Stoypa Sk'abelkohn's hair—pinned in two little buns atop her rosy round head—came up to the elf's eyes making her one of the few people she could look down on. And did she ever!

The dwarvish barmaid spoke to everyone as though they were adorable yet dim-witted babies, and the nasal whine of her voice made each saccharine syllable sound as though it were being wrung from her vocal cords, like syrup from a wet washcloth. She wore too much rouge, too many rings, and a forced abomination of a smile that looked as uncomfortable to wear as it was to observe. They walked the floor, the woman droning on about the subtle intricacies of serving patrons their food and ale, the Trow Elf's mind drifting to the myriad of ways she could kill the dwarf and leave no trace.

G'on, Jeydah, she thought. *You are* not *going to pock yourself over this time! Sure, it's a useless, demeaning shest bucket of a job, but*

Adam Berk

right now it's the only one you've got!

"And this is the service well," said the dwarf as they entered the sequestered area by the bar. "You'll stack your order slate here, the barkeeps will make your drink, and you'll make them look *bee-oo-tee-ful* before bringing them to your guests. Some garnishes take a little practice, but soon you'll be peeling twists like a master sculptor, *uh-huh, huh, huh!*"

Ye gods! Was that a laugh or an asthmatic goose dying of exhaustion?

"Next I'll have Garret go over our cocktails with you. Yoohoo, Garret!"

Jeydah, ever mindful of body language from her years stalking targets, noticed the large barkeep's neck and shoulders spasm at the sound of Stoypa cantillating his name. He glanced their way, nodded politely, and went back to talking to one of his customers.

"He's busying plying his charms, *uh-huh, huh, huh!* So, for now why don't we practice our carries, hmmm?"

The maître d' took a serving tray from a compartment by the bar and used a step stool to get ten empty wine glasses. She then loaded up the tray and handed it to Jeydah. The elf balanced it easily on one hand.

"Aww! Look at that, you're a natural!"

Jeydah gave the dwarf the widest fake smile she could muster.

I can throw over a hundred different projectiles with deadly accuracy, you annoying little sugar sprite. You think I can't—?

"Anyhoo, I've got to go give Master Wallingtok the reservations for tonight. You'll be training with Trina tonight. Isn't that perfect? I heard you two moved in together, so I'm sure it'll be *sooo* much better training with such a good friend! For now, you can just flob about with Garret and learn what you can about the cocktail menu. See you again when you cash out. Toodle-oo!"

Jeydah started to object that Trina was *not* a good friend, and was, in fact, one of the most infuriating vixes the elf had ever met, but Mistress Sk'abelkohn was already bustling off to

The Priestess & The Trow

the reception area. Over the past seven days, her flighty flatmate had found innumerable ways to test her, from her habit of taking food from the cold pot and leaving it in odd places around the flat, to her constant obsession with Demian wantcraft. Jeydah had always hated women who used their sexuality to get what they wanted. It was the antithesis of the strength and discipline she'd spent her last seventy-seven years developing.

Sighing, she grabbed the cocktail list and began committing its contents to memory.

"You'd do better to learn our inventory," said a deep voice beside her.

Jeydah looked up to see her flatmate's paramour, the Master Barkeep, Garret Stockwell peering at her through rows of hanging wine glasses.

"How much do you know about liquor?" he asked.

"I know which ones are best for masking the taste of certain poisons," she replied with a shrug. "Apart from that, not much. Never cared for the taste."

"I remember. You drink fefoni sours, right? That's what we in the business call a brass rapier: light and pretty but won't leave a mark. Come on back here, and I'll show you what's what."

Jeydah made her way to the entrance on the far side of the bar and joined the man behind it. Garret then alternated with easy grace between serving his guests and expounding on the differences of the inn's many varieties of liquor. The elf watched silently as he talked and worked, sorting the information into mental compartments where she knew she could retrieve it when needed.

She also took stock of the barkeep himself, trying to puzzle out what he and her pretty young flatmate saw in each other. He was a big man, with dark brows and a bristly goatee standing in sharp contrast to his shiny bald head. He could look imposing when the situation demanded, but at present his relaxed smile and deep, rumbling chuckles kept her and the patrons in affable spirits, even when some of them seemed determined to break the mood.

"Damn it, Stefan!" one man exclaimed. "No one wants to hear your ridiculous conspiracy theories. I was just telling my brother about the new Tellueric Temple in Frank."

"An' I'm tellin' you, tha's no temple! 'S a front for a dwarvish smuggling ring. Those li'l snollygosters in the Quartzite Valley're tryin' to import dreamstone without payin' those—waddya call 'em?—custodians!"

"Ho now, brahdas," said the barkeep. "No politics at the bar. You should know better. Anyway, Jeydah, the difference between a neutral spirit like kalein and a distilled infusion like gin is—"

Jeydah supposed she could understand a girl with intimacy issues like Trina using Garret as a reliable doormat while she had her wild flings at the Demian Temple. But what did the barkeep get out of it? Pretty faces were a cudgot-per-bushel in Angelwood, and he seemed far too pragmatic to mistake lechery for love.

Unless, she considered, he was having a mid-life crisis. Those always seemed to hit humans harder than other races with their brief sixty-to-seventy-year life spans. She noted the barkeep's scarred right hand and remembered Trina mentioning something about him originally wanting to be a blacksmith.

Jeydah felt an odd pang of sympathy for the big human. At 151 years, she'd reached the mid-point of her life as well. Here was a man who, like her, had assembled the fragments of his broken dreams into a makeshift shelter for the flurries of debilitations and disappointments mustered by advancing age.

"So, let me ask you something," she said, as Garret finished explaining the difference between light and dark rumbullion while stirring a Hupatali cocktail. "You and Trina are getting pretty serious, right?"

To her surprise, the man's entire head turned red as an apple in autumn.

"Well," he murmured through a sheepish grin. "It's all rather new, and we don't want to rush things, but I'd like to

The Priestess & The Trow

think we have a certain, special—oh, and you don't need to worry about Trina leaving her flat and moving in with me any time soon, if that's what you're wondering."

"Good to know."

She had been wondering that, but the main reason for her inquiry was of a more personal nature. Whatever else Garret might be, he was a good man, and if Trina truly was playing his emotions like an instrument, the elf thought she'd rather take her chances on the street, than accept any more of her charity. She couldn't live with someone she couldn't trust. Seventy-seven years with the Gardeners had given her a low tolerance for trollshest.

"But," she continued, "you're not bothered at all by her Demianism?"

"I was a bit at first, yes. I mean, what man wouldn't be? What with the wantcraft and the ritualized sex and all."

"What changed your mind?"

"The main thing was seeing what a difference it made in her. See, I don't want to say more than I should, but Trina's got certain—fears, that tend to muck up parts of her life. It comes from—well, let's just say she had some really rotpocked shest happen to her when she was younger."

Ah-ha.

Jeydah had suspected this. Trina hadn't gone into too much detail when she'd told her about her uncle, but it was clear the man had caused her some sort of traumatic pain. Long term emotional damage was one of the things the Gardeners had taught her to look for when evaluating a subject's calsahn. Their internal turmoil could turn them into either the best of heroes or the worst of monsters.

The furloughed assassin moved the barmaid out of the "annoying acquaintance" compartment in her mind, and into the one called "person of interest".

"I suppose," Garret continued after greeting a goblin couple and giving them menus, "that it's like when my kid sister Heora almost drowned. For the longest time, she wouldn't even dunk her head under the water when she was taking a bath. But then she started getting obsessed with fish. She'd learn about all the different kinds from fishermen at the market, even clean their skeletons and prop them up in displays around her room. We all thought it was weird, but it helped her get her head around her fear somehow, and in a couple of years she was jumping off Ballista Warf like the rest of us."

"I think I understand what you mean," said Jeydah.

Assuming you're equating swimming with sex and your sister's fear with some kind of intimacy issue you likely won't want to talk about.

He took the goblins' order and made their drinks. Then, having nothing further to do, he set about wiping surfaces and polishing wine glasses. Not liking the feel of standing idly by, Jeydah picked up a bar towel and followed the barkeep's example, watching him out of the corner of her eye. His behavior seemed fidgety, but she couldn't tell if it was from talking about his personal life, or the kinetic nature of his job.

So she decided to test it.

"But you do realize," she said as she casually wiped the back counter, "there's a big difference between taking a dip in the sea and having some random koudga puttin' his dipper in your honeypot."

There was a high-pitched crack. Jeydah looked up to see Garret glowering at two halves of a broken wine glass in his hands.

"It's not like that," he said putting the pieces in a bucket by his feet. "I've talked with the priestesses about it. When one of 'em takes the mantle of the Goddess, it's like she turns into a totally different person. The Goddess Demia, I suppose."

Suuure.

"From what I understand everything's so formal and ritualized it's not like real sex anyway. Long as she dun't take the Path of the Doorkeeper, heh-heh."

"What are *you* two talking about?"

Garret jumped as Trina popped into the service well behind him.

"Just showing Jeydah the basics of liquor service, li'l

The Priestess & The Trow

dove."

"Teedee koke, big bear. I'll take it from here."

In the next few minutes, Trina showed Jeydah the basics of table service: how the common room was divided into sections of six tables per server, how to walk in a continuous circle from your section to the kitchen, to the server's "alley" by the pick-up window and back, and how to present wine, coffee, tea, and some of the trickier entrees. All was delivered with quick-paced professionalism, and a smile so genuine, the elf began to suspect her feather-brained flatmate had switched places with a secret, sweet-tempered twin.

It's compartmentalization, she realized. *Gods know, I've had to separate my feelings from my work as an assassin, but these barmaids and dappers could teach me a thing or two!*

The evening rush hadn't hit yet, so Trina was demonstrating something called "steps of service" by an empty table, when a dapper caught her attention with a delicate tug on her blouse-sleeve.

"Ho, Trina!" he said, his voice low and lilting. "Sorry to be a bother, dollykins, but I'm in desperate need of your special talents right now!"

"Loris Patronus, you prassy vix!"

They kissed each other on both cheeks, as was the custom among the sophisticated gentry of Tyrn, or some of the more posh cliques of mollyboys in West Angel.

"I'm here for an hour," she said. "And you don't say one word to me. But soon as you pish up an order, I'm your best friend, is that it?"

"No! I've been slammed! Stoypa's been double seating me since night shift started. Says she dun't want to give you any tables 'til your trainee's been oriented."

"Ugh! Nice of her to tell me! I swear, I don't know what's going through that dwarf's mog sometimes."

"Gusts, zephyrs. Maybe a sylph or two. Anyway, I need you to get Kade to req a meal for one of my guests."

"If I must!" said Trina with a melodramatic sigh. "You know it'd be easier to get him to sell his left noddie than to give someone a free meal."

"I know," said Loris, throwing up his hands in dramatic chagrin. "The fussy elvish frepp at table twelve wanted his roast pheasant with plum sauce on the side."

"Wait," said Jeydah. "Did you just say 'wreck a meal'?"

"I know what it sounds like," said Trina with a laugh. "It's req. R–e–q. Short for requite. It's when a guest dun't like their meal, and the inn pays for it. Though asking Kade to sign for it can certainly 'wreck' a server's day. He usually assumes it's our fault for not checking the plate and takes the cost out of our tips."

"That's disgusting!"

"That's the Freelands. Garret says the Publican's Guild's been trying to keep proprietors from doing shest like that for decades but hasn't made much progress. Most servers in Angelwood are too busy auditioning for plays and minstrel jobs to go to guild meetings."

She shot Loris a look and he gave a little bow in response.

"Guilty as charged. Got a callback tonight for 'The Siege of Cynoc' over at the White Mountain Playhouse. Spent all night going over my lines and now I'm so muddlemogged I don't know if I'm setting or bussing."

"Case in point: looks like table twenty two is flagging you down."

Loris turned on his heel and sashayed over to a family of four whose infant son appeared to be using his spoon to catapult peas at his older sister.

Blacksmiths for barkeeps, Jeydah mused as she followed Trina to Kade Wallingtok's office. *And players for dappers. I'd wager there in't a single soul working here that wouldn't rather be doing something else.*

She found the thought comforting—as though she'd found some distant kindred that she never knew she had.

Kade's office was past the reception area, in the part of the inn furthest from the bar, the kitchens, the stage, or any other place where people might be having a good time. When Trina knocked, there was no response save the soft sounds of

The Priestess & The Trow

shuffling parchment. Finally, the door opened framing the proprietor's swarthy face and passive-aggressive, yellow-toothed smile.

"Hello, Master Wallingtok," said Trina. "Loris and I need a req on a roast pheasant on table twelve."

"No," said the proprietor. "You and Loris need to *pay* me for the cost of a roast pheasant on table twelve."

He started to close the office door, but the barmaid had wedged her shoe under the crack.

"It wasn't us. The guest forgot to tell us to put his sauce on the side."

Trina went on to explain how the guests were loyal customers, and oh so apologetic about the expense they were causing their favorite tavern, but one of them couldn't properly digest plums, you see, and—Oh no, no! Kade didn't need waste his time talking to them *personally!*

To the untrained eye, it would seem as though the barmaid were merely fidgeting as she spoke—a shifting hip, or a flutter-fingered gesture to dispel her discomfort at addressing her superior. But Jeydah had lived in Angelwood for fifty-seven years. She'd investigated the Temple of the Cavorting Incarnate at the Gardeners' behest, and even spoken with the Angelwood Chapter's founder, a prodigal fairy named Jane Forecroft. As such, she recognized every one of Trina's vocal intonations and gestures as coercive magic.

But what, she considered was the alternative? That poor, aspiring player paying for a fussy guest's meal out of his own pocket? Jeydah kept silent and watched in stoic fascination as the young Demian aspirant plied her craft.

"All right," Kade muttered in his bouncing Yllgoni accent.

He pulled a ponderous ledger off a shelf, flipped through several mostly blank pages, and made a notation on the one headed with current date.

"I am thinking I am remembering these two from their last visit. Good people. Very successful. Next time you will be telling me of them before they are halfway out the door, yes?"

Trina gave the proprietor a dazzling smile and a quick half

curtsy before returning to check on her section. Jeydah moved to follow, but Master Wallingtok caught her with a hawkish stare.

"You are the new barmaid, yes?"

Jeydah mimicked Trina's half curtsy. The movement felt about as natural as mounting a Gai-Autische dire rat.

"Trina assured me you'd be a good addition to our staff. She's a good barmaid, so I decided to be giving you a try tonight. But, am I understanding correctly that this is your first job in food service?"

"Yes, sir."

"And where was it you were working before?"

"I ran my own business as a woodcarver."

"I see. I assume it was unsuccessful as you are now training to work here."

Jeydah blinked, surprised by the man's callousness. *Is he trying to get a rise out of me?* If running a woodcarving shop had indeed been the most important thing in her life, she might have wept, yelled, or put a few gaps in that yellow-toothed smile of his.

"There were," she said coolly, "some guild conflicts I couldn't resolve."

"From what I am seeing, owners of small businesses are used to doing things their own way. They can perform many tasks efficiently, but are too rough with guests, making them feel talked down to instead of served. Are you thinking you might be acting this way with guests here?"

Only the stupid ones.

"No, sir. I understand I have a lot to learn."

"Good. See that you do."

Wallingtok gave a satisfied nod and reopened his office door.

"And thank you for taking a chance on me."

"Oh, I don't take chances," he replied, glancing over his shoulder with a smile. "You haven't signed an employment contract yet. If you don't impress me tonight, you don't work here."

The Priestess & The Trow

Well. Pock you too!

As the office door closed in Jeydah's face, she wondered in a flash of anger if the callous proprietor might be a good candidate for pruning by her fellow Gardeners. His removal would certainly benefit the calsahns of numerous barmaids and dappers. It was something to consider when she got back on good terms with her fellow assassins.

If she ever got back on good terms with them, that is.

She reentered the common room and found Trina hopping frantically between six full tables that had been empty moments before. Before the elf could say a word, the barmaid thrust an order slate in her hands and told her to take drink orders from the nearest party. The table had six burly young males—two goblins, two humans, a dwarf, and a satyr—proclaiming themselves stagehands enjoying a rare night off between rehearsal and production. She didn't recognize half the drinks they ordered, but she wrote them down as best she could.

Moments later she reconvened with Trina at the bar's service well. The barmaid pulled her into a nook between bustling servers and showed her with urgent efficiency how to write the table and seat numbers at the top of the slate. Then she looked over the elf's orders as sweat beaded on her finely lined brow.

"You also always want to ask if they want their niktalich cocktail with a cherry or peeled fuzzberry garnish. Also, what are jinanda rocks?"

"I was hoping you knew. He said he wanted a glass of orange juice and jinanda rocks."

"Gods and spirits! I can't teach you everything you need to know about serving *and* hop around six tables like a sylph in a cyclone. Stoypa!" she yelled over her shoulder. "What in the abyss were you *thinking* flat seating me like this?"

Jeydah saw the maitre d' standing awkwardly by the service area holding an armful of menus.

"Well," said the dwarf, "Everyone else's sections looked full, and I just thought since you had the extra hands tonight—

Adam Berk

uh-huh, huh, huh!"

Trina's faced flushed and contorted into a look of such murderous ire, that Mistress Sk'abelkohn scurried back to the reception stand as though a rabid dog were at her heals.

Such muddlemogged asininity, thought Jeydah. *How can anyone keep their sanity working here?*

"Trina, I'm sorry," she said, attempting to calm the exacerbated barmaid. "I'll go back to the table and ask the fellow what jinanda rocks are."

"Gin on the rocks."

They turned and saw Garret Stockwell standing behind the bar flipping through Jeydah's stack of service slates.

"These orders are pretty bad, but I've seen worse. You ladies go pre-set your tables. I think I can figure this out."

Trina took a breath as a smile of profound relief brightened her florid face. For a moment, Jeydah saw the burly barkeep through the barmaid's eyes: not a bald, paunchy, middle-aged frepp of a man, but a pillar of wisdom and sanity amidst the roiling tumult of the dinner rush. He chipped ice and lined up glasses in the service well, moving with the unshakable confidence of a hero in a ballad.

The rest of the night rushed by in a blur. Trina handled most of the order-taking and conversing, while Jeydah delivered food, and pulled dirty plates. The elf had to give the barmaid credit: she handled herself admirably under pressure. As unfocussed and flighty as she came across sometimes, she could still remember two dozen orders, keep drinks filled, and charm her guests, all without losing that dazzling smile.

It wasn't until the rush had died down, and the last of the guests were having dessert, enjoying digestifs, or sinking into drunken oblivion, that the problems started.

The woman was human, but big enough that Jeydah had to double check to make sure she didn't have the pointed teeth and pachydermal skin of an ogress. She sat by herself in a corner table, looking over the common room with the cold, black gaze of a sorceress surveying a newly indentured horde of demons. She caught Jeydah's eye and beckoned her over.

The Priestess & The Trow

"May I help you, Miss?" the elf asked. Her smile shifted on her face like an ill-fitting mask.

The woman frowned, ominous shadows over her heavy-lidded eyes, her downy jowls aquiver.

"Yes."

She paused, making a show of composing herself as though she were presenting a new article for the Moonflower Purchase. Jeydah, who saw the tactic for what it was—an attempt to make her squirm and feel subordinated—remained still and waited.

"I'm disappointed," the woman said at last, "that you took my plate without asking if I wanted it wrapped up."

Pockin' abis!

The idea of wrapping up meals for guests to leave with was a new one, and unique to the Freelands, where Syndraxan cold-pots were commonplace and Lascivian mages had means to manufacture and sell ice to the masses. Still, Jeydah, *had* asked the woman if she were done with her meal, and the patron had responded by turning a page in a book she was reading and making a shooing away gesture with her free hand.

"I'm sorry, Miss," said Jeydah, her smile starting to turn into a baring of teeth. "I did ask if you were done. I guess I misunderstood your response."

"You did no such thing."

Are you calling me a liar, you great quivering shest-pile? No, Jeydah, keep it together. You need this job, remember?

"Ah. Well. I suppose I could be remembering it wrong."

"I suppose so. I'd like my entrée taken off the bill, please."

What?

Jeydah's faux smile fell like a stone-struck bird.

The whole meal? That was brush pheasant and tesmet beans. It's the most expensive dish on the menu! Wallingtok'll fire me for sure!

"I don't think the proprietor will let me do that."

"Ex-*cuse* me?"

"Well, there was barely anything left on your plate, and—"

"You're new here, aren't you?"

"Yes, but—"

Adam Berk

From there, the woman explained, as though to a child, how she'd worked as a purveyor for restaurants for thirty years and knew more about "the industry" than Jeydah probably ever would. She listed nearly a dozen things the elf should have included in her steps of service, half of which Jeydah *had* actually done, and the other half, the former assassin couldn't imagine barmaids at the Dragonsbane doing for all the silver in the Freelands.

She can't expect me to put her napkin on her lap in the middle of a rush like we just had. And what in the Abyss is a pocking table crumber?

"At any rate, you really should be sure you know what you're doing before you start waiting on people. I'm sure it's the same with—what was it you did before?"

Jeydah would have loved nothing more than to tell the condescending patroness about her work for the Gardeners, but decided it wouldn't be worth the risk while she was on probation.

"I owned a woodcraft shop on Artisan Way," she said instead.

"Well, if you ran your business as lackadaisically as you serve your tables, I can see why you're where you are now."

"Where? Getting a quarter-cup lecture on food-service because I threw out three bites of cold pheasant?"

The words were out of Jeydah's mouth before she could take them back, but she was past caring. Hearing the slight about her former business for the second time tonight had pushed her over the edge and she'd be damned if she was going to let some—purveyor? What was that a professional pocking *shopper?*—talk down to her.

"I told you, it was more than just the leftover pheasant—which, at any rate, was going to be my lunch tomorrow. I told you, quality service is—"

"I'm sorry, your *lunch?*"

Something snapped in Jeydah.

"It was three bites!" she yelled. "I can see you're in need of some drastic dieting, but there's still a big damn difference

The Priestess & The Trow

between 'lunch' and three pocking bites!"

The woman froze, mouth open, eyes wide as a deer scenting a lion.

"You're making a big mistake talking to me like that," she huffed, quivering jowls turning a splendid shade of scarlet. "I know the owners of this place. I'm going to talk to your proprietor right now, and—"

"And tell him what? How your life is so pathetic—"

"—tell him you've not only ruined my experience tonight—"

"—you have to lecture barmaids about their jobs, when you've clearly never lifted a tray in your life?"

"—but tomorrow as well. They know me. They know I like eating half my meal here and the other half—"

"*Half!* Are you pocking delusional?"

Jeydah cast about until she spotted her section's bus-crate. Deep inside her, a primal voice howled in triumph. There, atop a pile of dirty plates, was the oaken bowl containing the remnants of the woman's pheasant!

Swift as a striking serpent, she rushed to the crate, grabbed the bowl, and slammed it onto the table in front her guest's incredulous face.

"There it is! Three bites, see? One, two three! That's if your great bovine kull dun't accidently *inhale* it in your sleep!"

A hand grabbed Jeydah's arm from behind, pulling her back. She spun, reflexively grabbing her assailant with her free hand, ready to break fingers. But it was only Trina.

"What in The Great pockin' Abyss are you *doing?*" the barmaid hissed.

Trina's fair skin blazed bright red, and her blue eyes bulged. Until that moment, the elf wouldn't have thought the girl capable of such an expression. For the first time in centuries, Jeydah was at a loss for words.

Ash and iron, what have I done?

"Go wait for me at the host stand, while I try and handle this!"

Jeydah slunk to the simple podium by the inn's

entranceway. Thankfully, the evening rush was over, and the maître d' had already left her post to go over the night's sales figures, or whatever it was maître d's did when they weren't flooding hapless barmaids' tables with clamoring guests.

My stupid temper pocks me again!

She watched as her guest railed at Trina. If the barmaid was using her Demian art now, it looked more like desperate placation than any wantcraft Jeydah'd ever seen. As the elf watched her flatmate and trainer sputter and nod, hands held out as though she could physically hold back the flood of bile spewing from her guest's gargantuan mouth, the certainty of her impending termination set in like frost on a cold pot.

There's no way Wallingtok won't fire me over this!

Not since she'd seen her mother dying in a Syndraxan prison had she felt so powerless.

If I can't do this job, what's left? My work as an assassin kept me from joining the Woodworkers' Guild and I'm far too old to be taken on as an apprentice. Have I really just turned myself into a beggar?

Finally, Trina returned to escort Jeydah from the host stand to Kade Wallingtok's office. Her manners and posture were collected and poised but her wide eyes and grinding teeth hinted at storms below the surface.

"Trina," said the elf, falling into step beside the barmaid. "I'm so sorry. I can't do a job where I can't fight back!"

"Bah," Trina sighed. "You *can* fight back, you just have to be smart about it. You have a good memory and you learn quickly. You'd be surprised how adaptable old skill sets can be."

"Tell that to Wallingtok!" Jeydah moaned. "He's looking for any excuse to fire me, and I gave him one. If you evict me, I won't blame you."

Trina held up a hand signifying she needed a moment to collect her wits, took a deep breath, and then released it as though she'd been holding all the demons in The Abyss in her lungs.

"Jeydah," she said. "If I evict you it'll be because you're an arrogant, self-righteous germophobe who judges everyone she meets by the first sound outa their snollyhole, *not* because of that self-entitled hell-cow sitting at your table!"

"But Wallingtok said—"

"I know what Wallingtok said. You think you're the first barmaid to go hedwig on a guest? We have ways of handling these things. Loris!"

She waved at the dapper, who promptly excused himself from the trendily dressed dwarf and fairy couple he was chatting up and sashayed over.

"What ho, vixes! How'd our newling hold up during the flat-seating fury of Stoypa the Stupid?"

"We'll flob about that later, dolly, I promise. Right now, I need you to back us up. We've got a baited boar situation on table twenty-four."

"Well," said Loris, with a dramatic sigh, and a toss of his perfectly coifed hair. "If I must!"

"Right," said Trina, turning back to her trainee. "Let's go, then."

They crossed from the host stand to Kade Wallingtok's office in six quick strides, where Trina rapped on the door urgently. The sound of parchment shuffling and Yllgoni-accented grumbling rose from inside, until at last the door snapped open, revealing the glaring eyes and bristling beard of the proprietor.

"Master Wallingtok," said the barmaid. "There's a customer complaint at table twenty four."

"Oh really." He slapped a hand down on his desk and rose to his feet as though ready to grab a cleaver and start turning servers into sandwich meat.

"I honestly don't know what her problem is." Trina spoke in a breathy, tremulous voice as she made her blue eyes as wide and guileless as a lamb's. "Jeydah's barely said two words to her all night, and suddenly this lady pulls me over and tells me my trainee's been saying the most bizarre and horrible things—"

"Were you being rude to a customer?" Wallingtok snapped, rounding on Jeydah. "Because, if you were, I swear

Adam Berk

by the seven waters—"

"Master Wallingtok!"

But before the elf could so much as flinch at the proprietor's fury, Loris bounded up to him. He clutched the man's wiry forearm as though it were a casting call-sheet for an audition with Symonde Lyonscall himself.

"I know you're busy, but as soon as you're done with whatever this is, we have *got* to talk about the woman on table twenty-four!"

"What? Table twenty-four, you say?"

The proprietor paused, the gears of suspicion visibly turning in his stygian little head.

"Yes!" Loris exclaimed. "She's *clearly* trying to finagle a free meal out of us. She's been flagging people down all night to tell them the most outrageous lies. She said she saw Dori Fletcher spitting in someone's soup, for gods' sake!"

"That is ridiculous!"

"Exactly!"

"Mistress Fletcher is my best barmaid!"

"I know!"

"She is never so much as taking a sick day! Her father was Trophican navy for gods' sake!"

"Right?"

"Thank you, Master Patronus. I am thinking I know just how to deal with this person now."

Wallingtok glanced at Gerald, the Inn's staveman, and motioned for the guardsman to follow him as he crossed the floor to talk to the woman at table twenty-four.

"That was clever," said Jeydah, as she watched the proprietor with bated breath. "But do you really think it'll work? I mean if the woman sorts out what we're doing—"

"Oh, she's past sorting anything out at this point." Trina draped a forearm over the hostess podium next to the elf. "She was already upset, but I peppered our last conversation with the sorts of phrases that push guests to the brink of insanity: 'Please stay calm.' 'Have you dined with us before?' 'Don't worry, it's all kokachoni.' Things like that."

The Priestess & The Trow

"So you push a guest into going hedwig so *they* look like the kullbung! Is that what you meant by a 'baited boar'?"

"Yep. Also, I told her your name was Dori Fletcher."

"Impressive."

And it was. Jeydah watched as the problematic guest raged at Master Wallingtok. The proprietor, unphased, told her to pay her bill and leave while Gerald loomed over his shoulder like a black armored mountain. The woman slammed the silver down on the table and stormed out the door in a huff. Wallingtok turned toward at the barmaids, motioned for them to get back to work, and returned to his office without giving the incident another thought.

As Trina showed her how to do sidework and tally up her sales from the day, Jeydah reflected that serving people was far more difficult than killing them. She also began to understand how practical Trina's Demian arts could be. As distasteful as she found the idea of charming people to get what you want, the elf had to admit there was an art to it. And in a byss-pit like this, you either learned that art, or lost everything.

~ III ~

"Whew! Hey folks, is it getting hot out here or did I set myself on fire again?"

Trina watched from her table as the street performer juggled eight lit torches before a captivated crowd on the Veneria Beach boardwalk. Siey dan Feyr, a trendy Tyrnish bistro, had overpriced food and servers that treated their guests as though they'd plopped off a manure cart, but its deck had a spectacular view of the crowded promenade, and the sandy beach beyond. As the juggler plied his trade, the sunset behind him glowed in fiery counterpoint to his flaming brands, while the darkening sky made the conflagrant light grow ever more entrancing.

He makes it look so easy, Trina thought. *Throw one, catch another, over and over and over again. But when I try to do that with the disparate parts of my life...*

Garret had wanted to take her out tonight. He'd bought tickets to a new play *Befraus* by Nasus Magros—a Medanite satirist she'd been raving about since last Goramir when she'd caught a scene from his play, *The Illusory Cuckold* at a matinee on Showcase Weekend. As this was her last night off before her initiation ceremony, they'd planned their evening months in advance as a night of romance and recreation before she

The Priestess & The Trow

began her studies as a novice.

But the week before, she'd made a crucial discovery. She'd been researching Demian wantcraft in the restricted section of the Angelwood University library when she'd found a rare tome at the bottom of a neglected box of overstock volumes. The book had revealed things about her religion that could change the course of her life. Things she needed to discuss with her *palacukra*—her temple-appointed advisor—tonight, and not a quarter cup later!

Sandals flup-flupped on the wooden planks of the restaurant's deck, bringing the barmaid's mind back to the present. She smiled as her mentor, Dahlaikruya Baritsuti (Sister Suti to her friends), returned to their table with two drinks. As it was mid-fall, Sister Suti wore the customary gold and orange sari over a crimson underskirt and black chest band. The colors brought a warm glow to her bronze Gimadran complexion.

"I noticed our dapper still hadn't come for our drink order, so I got these at the bar. You drink white wine, right?"

"Good memory! You'd make a better server than the one we have. I haven't seen him since he dropped the menus then scurried away like we had gonny rot."

Sister Suti smiled that soft-lipped smile of hers that made all who beheld it feel as though they were wrapped in a soft blankets—and made Trina feel self-conscious about her thin lips and pinched front teeth.

"I *did* used to work as a barmaid," the priestess laughed. "I'm sure you noticed, our faith is most appealing to people with service jobs."

"I suppose so. I haven't spent as much time at the temple as I'd like. All of it still feels so new to me. Especially with my initiation only two days off!"

"Yes, I know. It can be overwhelming. The temple used to insist on a full year and a day before promoting aspirants to novices, but now it's only six moons. I think they're trying to compete with that new Thaumatology religion that's getting so popular."

"Well, that's what I wanted to talk to you about! My

training: it's not just rushed, it seems like I skipped some important parts of it."

"Really? Like what?"

"Well, I was reading about the four padivatas—did I pronounce that right? I'm never sure—"

"That's right. PAH-dee-VAH-duh. It means instrument, creative medium, or livelihood."

"Right. Well, I read about a fifth one that no one—"

"Ho there, ladies!" a masculine voice interjected. "I'm here to deliver a serenade."

Thinking it was one of the many Veneria Beach street performers trying to scam them for money, Trina turned with a harsh dismissal on her tongue. Then she recognized her co-worker Farian Daringsford and cursed softly instead. The apprentice barkeep stood by their table, lute in hand, dark eyes twinkling above his vulpine smile.

"Ho, Trina! Heard you've got your initiation this Aniday. Thought I'd come over and contribute to the night's celebration."

"I'm not here to celebrate. I needed to discuss—"

Before Trina could say another word, Farian launched into a grand rendition of The Ballad of Demia and Incubaal: the foundational story of the Demian religion.

> *O gather close you blossoming maids*
> *And listen, one and all.*
> *While I sing of how the dancer tamed*
> *The great Lord Incubaal.*

"Okay, Fare. I appreciate the gesture, but this isn't the—"

> *The great lord gave a mighty feast*
> *Upon his mountain high.*
> *In the splendid halls of Adpha Yahn*
> *That sit above the sky.*

"Seriously stop."

The Priestess & The Trow

A thousand gods and goddesses
Where invited there to go,

"Farian!"

For the finest fare and spectacle
The world would ever—ow!

The barkeep-bard cut off when Trina kicked him in the shin. The barmaid looked around the patio and saw every head turned their way, including several passersby on the boardwalk. Farian could have an exceptionally loud singing voice when he wanted.

"Are you *trying* to get us thrown out of here?" Trina asked.

"Actually," said Jeydah Carver, suddenly appearing at Farian's side, "we were hoping to get one of these idiot dappers' attention. We've been here over a quarter cup and no one's even glanced in our direction!"

"You too, huh?" Sister Suti laughed. "Why don't you join us? I assume you're friends of Trina's."

That's using the term loosely, the barmaid thought with a grimace. She could enjoy the egocentric barkeep's company from time to time, but the Trow Elf was finding new ways to crack her kull her every day. Their last shift together, an eager young dapper had offered to refill the spice bowls on her tables for her. Jeydah had looked at Trina as though she'd told the boy to get on his knees and shine her shoes.

"Why not do that yourself?" the elf had asked. "The lunch rush is over; it's not like you have anything better to do."

"Jaikin likes doing things for me," she'd replied with a shrug. "So, I let him do them, that's all. What's wrong with that?"

"Oooh, nothing at all, *princess*. Nobility's been doing shest like that for centuries."

That little vix! I don't care if she did *kill people for a living, if she calls me "princess" one more time...*

But for now, Trina held her tongue as the pair joined them at the table. What were they doing there anyway? Sure, Jeydah never passed up an opportunity to criticize, but going out of her way to sabotage her chances with the Demian Temple was extreme even for her!

"So, Trina," said Farian, beaming his widest smile as Jeydah studied her menu. "Your initiation this Aniday's going to be a pretty big event, eh? You know what to expect?"

"Uh, just a general idea really," said Trina, looking to Suti for guidance.

"It will be in the grand courtyard," said the palacukra. "There are forty-seven aspirants each ready to pass through an appropriate rite of passage—what we call their kundha—for their padivata."

"Fascinating. And will there be any entertainment?"

"Oh, gods!" Jeydah snapped her menu's wooden cover closed and rolled her eyes in disgust.

"Well," said Sister Suti, "the temple organist will be there, and the priestesses on the Path of the Siren will be—"

"You pocking kullbung!" the elf exclaimed. "*That's* why you insisted on coming here for dinner! You didn't know shest about this place! 'Oh, but Jeydah, their Leatherfish Tapenade is the finest on Ardyn!' Trollshest! You just wanted to hustle up a minstreling job at the Demian temple!"

I guess that answers that, thought Trina, rolling her eyes.

"Not true! I've dined here many times. I'd only thought of it when you said…"

Trina smiled with relief as the two of them fell into a familiar bickering match—the barkeep using his elocutionary gifts to justify his selfish actions while the elf called him out on his trollshest. Jeydah wasn't trying to ruin her religious sojourn after all. The barmaid had doubtless mentioned her impending initiation at work during the week, and the information had set Farian's opportunistic gears to turning.

Trina was about to clarify the situation with her confused palacukra, when an attractive young man in a dapper's uniform interjected.

The Priestess & The Trow

"Does this mean you'll be combining parties?"

Trina met the server's eyes and opened her mouth, preparing to captivate the man with her wantcraft and coerce him into giving them better service. But Jeydah snapped at him preemptively breaking the spell.

"Oh, look who's decided to show up! Yes, we're sitting together now. It shouldn't be a problem since we've been here over fifteen drams without any of you muddlemogs getting us so much as a rotpocking flagon of water!"

"I'll have to tell the floor captain," he replied, turning on his heel and marching away as though his spine were made of hardened spindleoak.

"Wait! At least take our orders!"

"Wow," said Farian. "I never would've thought such a popular place would have such bad service."

Then on seeing Jeydah glaring at him: "Uh, that is—they were quite attentive *last* time I was—I mean *times*, of course. All the times I've come here they've been—well, I'm sure it must be under new management, or something."

"I think they're short staffed," said Trina, looking around. "So they're cherry picking the rich looking customers and ignoring the rest."

"Perhaps," said Suti, "this would be a good time to apply our craft."

"That's what *I* was thinking! Maybe we can link his prajja with *come-see-my-secret-treasure*, and bolster the bond with *you-can-be-my-guide*."

"Ah. Well, normally I'd agree, but I think *sisters-at-play* would be better than *you-can-be-my-guide*. Our dapper doesn't like women in that way."

"You can *tell* that?"

"Or," Jeydah interjected, "I could find the proprietor and give him a piece of my mind."

With that the elf sprang from her seat, crossed the patio, and entered the restaurant, hunched and gliding on the balls of her feet as though hunting prey.

"I don't think she'll have much success," said Sister Suti,

watching the departing Trow. "As we say at the temple, mead traps more sprites than vinegar."

"Which reminds me," said Farian. "If you've got all the minstrels you need, how about an extra barkeep?"

"Fare, give it a rest."

"Sorry, Trina. I suppose you'll want to get back to prepping for your paddyvaddy, or whatever it is you're doing on Aniday."

"Padivata," Sister Suti corrected. "It's one of four life-paths an aspirant can choose. There's the Mother, the Siren, the Changeling, and the Doorkeeper, each representing a different facet—"

"Except there isn't just four, is there?" Trina burst out. If she couldn't get her request in now, she feared she never would. "There's the Oracle on something called the Path of the Moon! I read about it in Laksmaba Gartaa's *Dance of the Goddess*."

She reached into a satchel by her chair and pulled out the leather bound tome. The barmaid had needed to use every Demian charm she knew to coerce the university librarian into lending it to her. As she hefted it onto the table, she thought she saw a look of consternation flicker across Sister Suti's face, but it came and went so quickly, she couldn't be sure.

"Wow," said the priestess. "That's a very old book. I'm surprised you were able to find a copy."

"It can't be *that* old. It's written in Gimadren but it's common letters, not pictographs. The empire's only used those for what? The last century or so?"

"Yes, well—things move swiftly in the Freelands."

"So," said Farian, refusing to be shut out of the conversation. "What makes this Moon Path so special?"

Trina shot her palacukra an apologetic look on behalf of her pushy friend.

"Well," said Sister Suti with a tolerant nod toward the apprentice barkeep, "do you know how each of the paths represents a different way of channeling one's prajja?"

"Prajja. That's some kind of sex energy, innit?"

The Priestess & The Trow

"We would say the attractive force of life."

"Right," he replied. "And if you want to be an actress, or a dancer you take the Path of the Changeling. Singers and musicians do the Path of the Siren, priestesses are the Mother, and, uh, well, heh-heh! I'm not really sure what Doorkeepers are other than the best time you'll ever—"

"The purest expression of our faith," the priestess interrupted. "Theirs is the most revered and powerful path, as it requires the total surrender to prajja in all its manifestations."

"As you say, sister," Farian laughed. "All I know is, last Doorkeeper I met did things to me you'd—"

"Back to the Moon Path," Trina grated. "The book says it's a path of scholarship. It studies and councils the other paths without being bound to the parameters of any of them."

"Yes," said Sister Suti. "And in our early days, Oracles of the Path of the Moon were essential, but now—"

"What're we talking about now?" asked Jeydah as she rejoined the group, turning her seat back-to-front before she sat in it. "I heard somebody mention the Moon Path. That's actually a good idea for you, Trina. I'd forgotten the Demians had that option."

There was a moment of stunned silence as the three of them turned to the elf. She moved swiftly and quietly and the priestess and the barkeep-bard were taken off guard by her sudden reappearance. Trina, who was used to her roommate's stealthy ways, merely waited for Jeydah to follow up her comment with some snide jab at the barmaid's religion or character.

For once, the remark did not come.

Sister Suti was the first to speak.

"You're familiar with the Demian faith, then?"

"You could say that."

"Sister, please," Trina cut in. "I really think I need to change my padivata! If what I've read about the Moon Path is true—"

"No one," said the priestess, "has taken the Path of the Moon in almost a century. I'm sorry, little chica bird. Even if the temple did still offer that way, I wouldn't know the first thing about it."

"That's what happens," said Jeydah, "when a religious hierarchy suppresses information."

"What do you mean?" asked Trina.

"I've lived in Angelwood for nearly a hundred years, you know. I remember when your high priestess met in secret with the librarians' guild to rid the region of 'misleading literature'."

"Is that true?" Trina asked Sister Suti. "Are writings about The Path of the Moon considered 'misleading literature'?"

"Certainly not!"

"Then why is a book like this in the restricted section?" asked Jeydah, hefting the volume. "You said yourself it's not that old, and it's in excellent condition."

"Plus," said the barmaid, "there are books referenced in *Threading the Wheel* and *Dancing with Desire* that I haven't been able to find anywhere!"

The priestess gave a helpless laugh, throwing up her hands in response.

"I can see why you two are friends. You play off each other better than the impromptu players at the Upstanding Civilians Company."

Friends? Trina glanced at the Trow elf who met her gaze and turned away with a dismissive sniff. *You've got to be joking.*

"Anyway," the priestess continued. "The idea of the Temple of the Cavorting Incarnate pressuring librarians to ban books is ridiculous. We're a humble religious order. We've never had anywhere near that much—What's the word?—*clout* with the community."

Jeydah opened her mouth to retort, but was interrupted by a portly man in a fine black tunic running up to their table.

"*Pran mon lescuse,* my friends," said the man, his words slurred in a syrupy Tyrnish accent. "But you are Demian priestesses, no?"

"I am," said Sister Suti. "And this young lady's being initiated in two days."

"*Mon dhu!* And to think what awful service my worthless

The Priestess & The Trow

excuse for a dapper was giving to you! I am horrified. Please allow me to take your orders. Everything will be on the house!"

Sister Suti nodded graciously in response, as though such deferment were the most natural thing on Ardyn.

That's clout if I ever saw it! Trina thought, but decided not to press the issue. She glanced at Jeydah and the Trow gave her a sly smirk, telling the barmaid she was thinking the exact same thing.

The barmaid decided she'd pay the temple a visit tomorrow before her shift and attempt to glean information about the Path of the Moon from the high priestess Majjikphima Hilanda. If the woman evaded her, she resolved to postpone her initiation, perhaps indefinitely. The thought was so disappointing it made her ache, but if her temple was being this manipulative with their aspirants, well, she'd had quite enough of *that* sort of thing from her noble parents and lecherous Uncle Shosev, thank you very much!

The rest of the meal was pleasant enough. They had wine and Cúir Riolases, *pheasant críbon guer* and leatherfish tapenade. The conversation moved from Demian theology, to ballads, to favorite sirens and Pit fighters.

The owner insisted not only on paying for everything but serving them himself so even tipping wouldn't be necessary. Trina still left four silver coins on the table on principle, though she was careful not to let Jeydah see it. "Always need everyone to like you, don't you?" the little trow would have jeered.

Trina said goodbyes to her friend Farian, her palacukra and whatever annoying thing Jeydah was in her life and contemplated what to do with the rest of her day. Since she had a bit more silver in her purse than expected, she haled a harkey cart and left to spend the rest of her day off at the Angelwood University library.

When she got there, she glanced through a front window to see who was behind the front desk. It was Filbert, the student she'd charmed into letting her take *Dance of the Goddess* from the restricted section a few days prior. As the barmaid wasn't ready to either return the book, *or* make good on her promise to let Filbert show her "the perfect spot on campus to drink wine and watch the sunset", she left the front stoop in favor of a side door opening into a reading room, with castle-like stone walls, a high ceiling and stained glass windows.

Cautious as a heretic in a temple, she rushed through the room before the students hunched at the long, divided tables noticed her. Once among the labyrinthine array of bookcases, the familiar smells of aging glue and paper did much to calm her nerves. After a few familiar twists and turns, she found the shelf she wanted: the collected myths and folktales of Old Gimadra. She grabbed two books she hadn't read before, and three that she had, sat on a stool wedged inconspicuously in a corner and began to flip through them.

For a cup and a half, she read and skimmed and read again, looking for any old tale or legend that might give her clues about the Path of the Moon. The best she could find, however, was a story about Demia and the Moon Goddess, Duncandra, who first battled the younger deity then acted as her mentor, claiming the fight was merely a test and rewarding her with a magic mirror. The story was engrossing, and she spent the largest part of her time reading it, but by the end she felt more confused than ever.

By the time her harkey cart took her back to her building, it was well past sunset. She was not surprised to see oil lamps burning in her front window. Jeydah kept late hours woodworking, meditating and doing gods-knew-what in her sectioned-off corner of the flat. Trina was surprised, however, when she walked through the front door and found the elf sitting at the table, her miffin on her lap, flipping through the barmaid's copy of *Threading the Wheel*.

"This is a later edition than the one I read. There's a lot they left out."

Trina made an exasperated noise.

"Could you *not?*"

She stomped across the floor and snatched her book out

The Priestess & The Trow

of her flatmate's hands. Rhys lifted a wing and half rose as though considering flying to his mistress' defense. But he opted to clean his beak on the edge of the table instead.

"Bad enough you have to metaphorically rip apart my beliefs, I don't need you doing it physically, too!"

"All right! Truce!" said Jeydah, holding up her hands. "*I* don't destroy books, unlike those priestesses of yours."

Trina glared at her as she carried her book back to its proper place in her bookcase. She hated to admit it, but she was beginning to suspect the elf was right about the Demians suppressing information.

"You seem to know a lot about the temple for someone who hates them so much."

"Hate's a strong word," said Jeydah.

She stood and walked to the hearth. Rhys trilled in protest as he hopped to the floor.

"They irritate me," Jeydah continued. "I think they're a bunch of social climbers and hypocrites. But everyone's entitled to their own stupid beliefs as far as I'm concerned."

Like murdering people because a bunch of forest dwelling fanatics say it's for a higher purpose, Trina wanted to say. But she kept her mouth shut. After all, if the Trow elf did know something about Path of the Moon, this might be the barmaid's only chance at getting the information she needed.

"I know a lot about them," Jeydah continued as she filled the teakettle and stoked the embers beneath it, "because their founder, Jane Forecroft was a person of interest to the Gardeners back when Demianism was still in its formative stages. You want tea?"

"Yes, please," said Trina.

The barmaid was already setting the table with cups, plates, a small tray of biscuits and a jar of fuzzberry preserves. Over the past two weeks, tea had become an unofficial parlay flag between them. No matter how mad the elf's snide remarks would make Trina, or how irate Jeydah would get at the barmaid for leaving clothing and dirty plates strewn about the flat, the one thing they could always count on was mutual civility over cups of tea.

"There are some people in the world," said Jeydah as she measured dried herbs into their tea pot, "whose calsahn could either heal the world, or break it entirely. Your temple's founder was one of those."

Trina nodded. Jeydah had explained the guild of assassins' concept of "calsahn" to her and her friends during a more amicable time in their relationship. It was similar to the Demian concept of padivata, but without as much free will involved.

"Well," said the barmaid, "I take it High Priestess Forecroft passed muster with you people. Since she lived to a ripe old age and left a thriving religious organization behind her."

"She did. Although," the kettle's whistle swelled to an insistent shriek, and the elf paused to pour the hot water into the teapot. "One of my last directives before my suspension was to keep an eye on your current Majjikphima. She's been running your temple more like a commercial enterprise than a religion. Expanding recruitment operations, cutting initiation procedures, consolidating official responsibilities—'streamlining' is what merchants would call it."

"Probably because The Church of Thaumatology's been poaching so many of our aspirants," Trina postulated. "Okay, so Demianism's going mercantile like everything else in the Freelands. Why should that worry anyone?"

"That's a question for the *frémina*—the Gardiners' Council of Roots."

Jeydah brought the teapot to the table and sat across from the barmaid as they helped themselves to biscuits and preserves while the herbs and tea leaves steeped.

"They'd probably say that channeling power—in your case prajja energy—back to its source creates an ethereal feedback loop, or some esoteric mumbo jumbo. I say, when a group uses people's primal drives for profit, bad things happen."

Trina poured herself some tea. She normally let it steep for a full six drams, but right now she needed something to do

The Priestess & The Trow

with her hands. The idea of her temple using the sacred rite of her goddess as some sort of commercial scheme did not sit well with her.

"Assuming that's what's going on," said the barmaid, "what would it have to do with the Path of the Moon or disappearance thereof?"

"Consolidation of power," said Jeydah, taking a bite of a biscuit. "Followers of the Moon Path were the true mystics of the religion. They were responsible for spiritual guidance, while priestesses on The Path of the Mother handled temple administration, public relations, and more mundane affairs. Now the mystics are gone, and the Mothers are in charge of everything from public policy to the spiritual journeys of their charges."

Here the elf paused, poured a small measure of tea, and tasted it, holding it in her mouth with a contemplative expression. She then gave a satisfied nod, and poured herself a cup, sweetening it with several dollops of honey.

"Don't look so distressed, this sort of thing's common in religion. As the institution grows, it becomes less about spiritual experience, and the more about exploiting its members. So, you gotta ask yourself, is your journey with the goddess real enough that you'd swim through a political cesspool to complete it?"

Trina sat back in her chair, considering. The Temple of the Cavorting Incarnate certainly had its dark side now that she thought of it. She'd seen how the priestesses manipulated prominent councilmen, guild leaders, and impresarios: plying them with fine food, strong drink, and transcendent sexual experience before striking deals with them behind closed doors.

But she couldn't forget her own transcendent experiences with the Goddess Demia, either—especially that time in her Uncle Shosev's fairy grove when she'd used her powers to drive him to madness and out of her life. She knew her wantcraft was more than just playing on people's desire. With every rhupa she learned, she felt the presence of the goddess grow inside her, replacing the terrified little girl she used to be.

"Yes," she said at last. "I don't care how much this ridiculous polis is corrupting Demianism. The goddess *is* real to me. She's the most real thing in my life!"

"More real than what you have with Garret, even?"

"What we have is love. The goddess *is* love."

"Heh. Hopefully *he'll* see it that way. Anyway, your high priestess might be turning your religion into a common brothel, but there's a good chance representatives from other temples will be there tomorrow as well. That means the ceremony will still have to meet certain standards, including offering a chance to take the Moon Path. What you want to do is—"

"Hold a drop. Why are you taking such an interest in this anyway?"

Trina studied the elf suspiciously. If this was part of some Gardener plot…

"You taught me how to be a barmaid," Jeydah said with a shrug. "Seems only right that I return the favor."

The elf stared into her teacup as though she could read the leaves. And maybe she could, Trina realized. Whatever the message, it didn't seem to be welcome news.

It's hard when you're kept from doing the thing you love, thought the barmaid. *Must be even harder when you've been doing that thing for over a century.*

"Maybe our calsahn's are interwoven," Jeydah continued. "Or maybe the spirits are pocking me again."

"Well, okay. As long as I don't end up killing anybody."

"Perish the thought. Now, the Demians always intended the Path of the Moon to be a secret, but one that a more studious initiate could figure out in the course of her studies. So the way they arranged it was…"

Jeydah lectured on, telling Trina all she knew about her religion's secret padivata. The barmaid listened, elation filling her heart not only from the ancient wisdom she was learning but also that her new flatmate, for once, was talking to her with a measure of respect. Though she'd never admit it, it was the

The Priestess & The Trow

second reason that made her smile.

~ IV ~

"I say! You're a Trow, aren't you? I don't usually see *your* kind in this line of work."

The Ljolas Elf was gaunt, even by the standards of his folk, and wore a blindingly white chemise under a striped gold and green jerkin. The garments looked as though he took better care of them than he did himself. He sat with two humans and a dwarf, all male and all dressed in similar finery. His name was Svaheil Seinerviche, and the other barmaids had warned Jeydah that he was fussy as an infant, pompous as a peacock, and condescending as, well, a gold elf dining in the dingy common room of the Dragonsbane Inn.

"Yes, sir. I had a woodcraft shop until recently, but it went under. Had some trouble with the—"

"Enough, girl, I didn't ask for your life's story."

He cut her short with a dismissive wave of his thin-fingered hand. Jeydah took a deep breath and tried not to think about how easy it would be to jam a butter knife into the back of his scrawny neck.

"Now," Svaheil continued, "I'd like to select a bottle of Glannadrey to complement our roast pear and goat cheese on flatbread, but I need to know—what is the goat cheese's country of origin?"

The Priestess & The Trow

"It's locally sourced, sir."

Jeydah didn't know for sure, but she knew Master Walligtok was far too cheap to buy imported products if he didn't have to.

"Ah-ha. I see. And what region in particular?"

"Central West Coast. South of Frank. A small farm just outside Kingsmount."

This was completely made up, but she couldn't bring herself to go scurrying to the kitchen and back with the elf's pointless questions. Business had been slow her first two shifts and she was beginning to worry she might not make rent. Svaheil's companions seemed similarly impatient, as she noticed exchanged smirks and eye-rolls passing between the humans, and the dwarf glowering and muttering into his beard.

Svaheil, oblivious to this, continued to study the wine list with great solemnity as he delved the depths of his gastronomic wisdom. He stroked his narrow chin, licked his thin lips, and crinkled his pale brow, as though he were a diplomat between warring nations and the parchment tacked onto a plank of stained pine in his hand, a long-sought treaty, until…

"Were the goats grain fed or grass fed?"

"Oh, for the love of dirt!" the dwarf burst out. "Nobody cares about the pockin' goats, you great prassy poof! Stop preening your feathers and pick the cheapest one like you always do!"

Jeydah had to bite her lip to keep from laughing. Most elves, particularly the Ljolas or "gold" types like Svaheil, didn't care for dwarves. They thought they were grimy uncouth creatures, misshapen by generations of working underground. It was testament to the dwarf's status in The Wyte and Golde Building Company that Svaheil was spending any time with him at all.

Trow like Jeydah, choosing to wander the world in nomadic tribes rather than hiding themselves away in forest communities, were less stuffy than their fair-haired cousins. Seeing this dwarf call the gold elf out on his trollshest, she felt a growing affection for the shaggy haired little fellow. After taking the rest of their orders, she shot him a wink and was rewarded with a smile as he hefted his tankard in her direction. And if that wasn't enough to lift her spirits, the look on Svaheil's face—veins bulging along his receding hairline, the cords of his chicken neck taught as lute strings as he ordered the *second* cheapest bottle of Glannadrey—certainly did the trick.

Maybe this job isn't the same as shoveling shest for diarrhetic demons in The Abyss, after all, she thought. She dropped her order slate at the bar then side-stepped to the food-prep area to assemble a basket of bread. *There's a routine to it with enough variety to keep from becoming tedious, and most problems are easily fixed or delegated without the fate of nations hanging in the balance.*

But even as she took comfort in her newfound skill, she could see how the life of a barmaid would eventually grind her down. Already she missed her work as an assassin: traveling to interesting places, making a difference in the world, running her woodcraft shop under Gardener patronage so she could be as rude as she wanted to customers she didn't like. If the guild of assassins refused to take her back after her probation, she worried that she could be stuck bowing and scraping to the likes of Svaheil for decades. The thought made her want to howl like a lone wolf in winter.

She put the bread on a tray, then returned to the bar for her drinks. Trina stood in the service well talking to Garret. Jeydah was about to push past to get her drinks but then reconsidered. The couple weren't engaged in their usual flirtatious banter, but rather something lower, and much more prickly.

"Fine then," the barmaid grated. "If your position here is *so* important to you, I guess I'll just sell my soul to the Angelwood playhouse companies."

"It's not that at all," the barkeep shot back. "I just don't like the idea of suddenly moving to a whole new polis because you heard *their* Demian priestesses might be a bit less bosky than ours!"

The Priestess & The Trow

"It's not suddenly! It'd be after a year as a novice. You could plan our move to your great freppish heart's content."

"Oh, I'm sure I could! I'll end up handling all the logistics while you're too busy juggling all the studying and chores of a novice with your work at the inn to be any help at all."

"Oh, logistics, is it? Don't be dramatic, it'd be just up the coast to Frankton. Or down to Crown Harbor, if that's too far for you to manage."

"Distance isn't the issue, it's—look, I've got other guests to attend to. We'll discuss this later."

"Wait! You haven't poured my hupatali yet!"

Garret slammed the cocktail glass onto the service bar, and the stem broke in his hand. Muttering curses he grabbed another glass and sloshed the drink into it. Before either of the women could ask if he was alright, he humped down to the other end of the bar to pour two tankards for a boisterous goblin couple with wide, tusked smiles and green skin flushed to a grayish brown. Trina shot Jeydah an exasperated eye-roll and returned to her tables.

The elf had served her drinks, then returned to the food prep area where her flatmate was cramming butter into ceramic ramekins for the impending dinner rush.

"Pocking men!" Trina fumed. "Pass laws saying only *they* can own property or get a seat on the polis council. Tell themselves *they* know everything, then start chucking buckets when you prove 'em wrong."

"Trouble with the paramour?"

The girl shook her head as though she didn't want to talk about it. Then, just as Jeydah turned back toward the common room, she spun about with an exasperated noise.

"All I did was mention that I might want to move in a year or two and he started huffing and moaning like a bear with a bellyache."

"Hmm. Sounds like he's not as comfortable with your Demianism as he lets on."

Trina put the lid back on the butter pot and fixed the elf with a level stare.

Adam Berk

"You think I'll have to choose between Garret and my religion, don't you?"

"That would be something to consider, yes."

"I don't think it'll come to that," said the barmaid, shaking her head. "Garret's more understanding than that. We have to find the time to talk things out, that's all."

"Okay. But what if it does? Come to that, I mean."

"Well," she said, lowering her eyes with a heavy sigh, "then I'd miss him dearly. Leaving him would be hard as cutting off a finger, but I could never stay with a man who wouldn't let me use my gods-given gifts. You have to go where your heart leads, you know?"

Jeydah could only nod in response as the barmaid hustled through the kitchen door to return the butter to the cold room.

"Where the heart leads". Spoken like a true nobleman's daughter! The heart is a selfish bastard who couldn't care less if the rest of the body dies. Only place you have *to go is where there's silver to be earned, and people aren't trying to pock you over at every turn.*

Turning back to the common room, the Trow Elf saw to her relief that business was picking up. Crowds of guests bottle-necked at the front door, and a new party sat bantering at one of her tables: a pleasant pair of couples dressed for a night out on the town. They ordered a bottle of their most expensive white, a Tyrnish fiángon blán, and Jeydah immediately started feeling better about her finances.

No sooner had she brought the order slate to the bar, however, than six black-armored stavemen entered the inn. A collective groan rumbled through the common room. Patrons shifted in their seats as though searching for inconspicuous ways to bolt from the building. For a moment, Jeydah thought the guardsmen might only be after a bit of refreshment between assignments, but then she saw how they filtered through the room questioning patrons. Her heart sank as she realized this was one of the Protector's Guild's raids she'd heard the other servers complaining about.

"So much for making any money tonight," Garret groused from the service well.

The Priestess & The Trow

"How often does this happen?"

"It's getting worse. This is the third time this moon."

"Seriously? What are you people doing, selling swords and sunder hexes in the basement?"

"They've been up our kulls ever since an angry centaur crippled two officers here last year. The Protector's Guild tried to amend Master Wallingtok's contract so he paid more. Kade refused. Now they do this."

The barkeep gestured to the other end of the room where a staveman was pulling the dwarven merchant at Jeydah's table to his feet.

"Disorderly conduct!" the dwarf raged. "Are you mad? I'm just sitting here!"

"As you say, sir, but we heard several anonymous witnesses state they saw you yelling at passersby and urinating in the adjacent alleyway."

"Trollshest! You can't do this to me! Do you know who I am? My crystal mines supply more than half this city's thaumacraft industry!"

"Then I'm sure you'll have no trouble paying the fine."

What a bunch of arrogant kullbungs! Jeydah fumed.

She watched the display with growing outrage. This was everything she hated about the Freelands: the constant bullying, extortion, and lies.

Still, she reminded herself. *This is the way things are done here. It's not just, but doing what you thought was right is what brought you to this sorry state in the first place. Keep your head down and your temper checked. It'll all be over soon.*

"If I can have everyone's attention, please."

One of the stavemen—apparently the leader of the band, though his armor was devoid of any rank signifying marks or adornments—stood on a chair and addressed the crowd.

"We've been getting reports of servers selling contraband from this establishment, so some of you folks will have to answer some questions."

Another groan rumbled through the crowd. Jeydah's lips curled in a snarl as her hatred for these black-armored jackasses burned hotter and hotter.

"That's a new one," said Garret shaking his head. "Someone better tell Kade."

Apparently, someone had, as on the other side of the room, the proprietor's office door burst open and wiry little man strode across the room, his dark features pinched and ashen. He approached the guardsmen's leader and the two immediately fell into a low-spoken flurry of haggling.

"We're willing to go as low as forty cenmarks."

"Those rates are absurd!" Wallingtok hissed. "Look at this place! Do you think I am serving the Emperor of Gimadra in here?"

"If we go any lower, you'll have to give us information on some of your guests."

"Which will be giving us a reputation as a 'stavebar' and driving my profits even lower!"

Jeydah'd heard enough. Throwing her order slate to the floor with a slap, she strode to the arguing men. She wasn't sure what she was about to do, but she'd spent most of her life ridding the world of trollshest. She knew she'd come up with something.

You have to go where your heart leads. Trina's words danced through her head, bringing a grim smile to her lips.

"G'on, Master Wallingtok!" she interjected. "Don't try to negotiate with these kullbungs. They're squeezing you in a protection racket, and they know it."

"Miss, this is a private negotiation between your proprietor and the Protectors' Guild. I don't know who you think you are, but—"

"Who I am, you great byss-blighted buckethead, is someone who's fed up with you swaggering shestmogs waving your big wooden stalks around like you're ready to pock the whole rotpocking polis!"

Hot anger coursed through her making her lips flap like banners in a firestorm.

"I'm someone," she raged on, "who's been fighting for justice since you were a drop of sparge in your momma's

The Priestess & The Trow

honeypot! I'm—"

The insight came in a flash.

"I'm your *competition!*"

The stavemen laughed uproariously. She'd expected that. After all, she was a lone elvish woman claiming to be better for the inn's security than a unit of trained fighters twice her size.

"Sir," said the guardsman, wiping his eyes, "you're free, of course, to hire independent security if you want. But I should warn you, the Protectors' Guild standards are—wait, what in the abyss is—?"

His quarterstaff wiggled in his hands as though coming to life. Staring perplexedly he shifted his grip as it twisted and writhed, spindle oak fibers crackling like the tendons of a long dormant limb. Then, all at once, it snapped backward into his crotch, breaking his codpiece with a resounding crack. He fell to his knees.

Jeydah snapped out of her trance, pulling her awareness back from the staff, but keeping her woodcraft powers at ready.

Kade Wallingtok shot her a measuring look. "I thought you said you were a shopkeeper."

"That was my cover. My real work was for an international mercenary company. I can protect your inn better than any of these leatherheads and for half the price."

Kade studied her a moment, fingers steepled in front of his pursed lips. Patrons and employees alike watched the exchanged with bated breath, and boots pointed toward the nearest exit. The only sounds were the carts on cobblestones of Angelwood Boulevard, the occasional furtive whisper, and the moans of the bludgeoned staveman as he writhed on the floor reeds.

"Interesting," said the proprietor. "And I assume I'd have to be hiring some of your mercenary friends as well. After all, you wouldn't be wanting to work nine days a week, would you?"

"I know some people," said Jeydah.

She didn't, but out of work mercenaries weren't hard to

find. She'd had several assignments, now that she thought of it, that had made use of such people.

"Go on!" bellowed the tallest staveman in the squad: a lantern-jawed brute who looked like he ate baby kittens for breakfast. "This little vix uses elven woodcraft, gets in a cheap shot on Dolph, and you think she's Ardath pocking Dragonsbane?"

Jeydah dropped into a fighter's crouch. She turned her face slow and steady to meet the guardsman's eye.

"Are you calling me a liar?"

"Worse. I'm calling you a bloody *scab!*"

The word visibly resonated with the other stavemen as they tossed down their quarterstaffs and drew sod-rods from their belts—stout black clubs designed for close combat. They were made of pure iron, she realized with a shudder. Iron was a well-known weakness for elves. Its touch caused their flesh to blister and burn.

An icy surge of self-doubt welled up inside her as patrons bolted from their tables clearing a space in the middle of the common room. There were six of them: well trained, armored and armed. As an assassin she was used to having the element of surprise in a fight, and never against such intimidating odds.

You'd be surprised how adaptable old skill sets can be.

And there it was again—Trina's voice in her head, saying the things Jeydah didn't want to hear but needed to.

Yep. Interwoven calsahns, she thought, shaking her head.

The guardsmen rushed her, and she released her fears, focusing instead on fighting techniques honed over decades of training. She lunged at the nearest stavemen, fists raised to strike his face. He raised his club and she dropped into a sliding kick. His knee popped beneath her heel and he tumbled into his comrades.

Taking advantage of their distraction, she sprang to her feet and scurried backward, catching herself on the edge of the bar. She slipped into a light trance, and reached out with her mind, throwing her awareness into the nearest discarded staff. Focusing her will, she willed the wood to bend backward, then

The Priestess & The Trow

released causing it to snap straight. The momentum sent it end over end into her outstretched hand.

She emerged from her trance, in time for the guardsmen to close in, trapping her against the bar in a tight semi-circle. With brutal precision, they took turns lunging at her two or three at a time. Heart racing, she whipped the staff every which way blocking most of their strikes.

Most, but not all. Hard iron burned her skin as it bruised her arms, legs, and back. One struck her forearm so hard it cracked the bone.

I will not cry out, she thought as the pain drove her to her knees. *Whatever these pockers do to me I will not scream.*

She looked up and saw the ugly, lantern-jawed face of the tall guardsman leering down at her. Then she blinked as a bottle smacked across it spattering glass everywhere. The staveman reeled backward with a howl, his visage a mask of blood and cheap whiskey.

A glance sideways revealed Garret, grinning and holding the broken neck of a shusheng bottle.

Their line broken, the stavemen hesitated for an instant. Jeydah seized that moment to press her advantage, breaking one's nose with the butt of her staff then vaulting onto the bar. Another tried to swipe at her legs, but she flipped over his head, landed at his back and broke his knee from behind.

Knowing she had only moments, Jeydah rushed the remaining three guardsmen. One got his teeth knocked out by her staff as he turned. A second fell choking with a jab to his larynx.

But the third grabbed her from behind. He locked her in a chokehold, iron club crushing her throat. Her neck exploded in white hot pain. She clawed at the metal but only scalded her fingers in the process. Her vision darkened and her lungs began to convulse from lack of air.

A solid thump sounded from behind her captor's back. His grip on her loosened—not a lot, but enough for her to jam her thumb under his metal bracer. She found a pressure point on his wrist and squeezed. The club slipped from his fingers.

Adam Berk

She lunged forward, freeing herself.

She whipped around in time to see the staveman fall to his knees. A squat figure assaulted him with a peppermill swung like a war hammer. Her rescuer flashed her a bearded grin, and she recognized the dwarven merchant. Before the guardsman had a chance to recover, he wacked the man in the face, sending his helmet flying in a cloud of finely ground pepper.

Jeydah smiled her thanks to the dwarf, then dropped back into a fighter's crouch, staff held in front of her ready to strike her next opponent. But then she saw the crowd around her had come to life. Emboldened by the stavemen's injuries, patron and server alike mobbed the guardsmen, shoving and kicking them toward the door with raucous jeers.

In moments the elf found herself mobbed by her co-workers. They laughed and cheered at ear-ringing volumes, clapped her on the back and hugged her a hundred different ways. Jeydah laughed along, elated but overwhelmed and even a little scared. She'd never experienced anything like this in her life.

A plump little hand grabbed hers and pulled her away from the crowd. Stoypa Skabblekohn, red-faced and beaming, shouted above the din that Master Wallingtok wanted to see the elf in his office. Jeydah followed her there, thinking that the dwarven Maitre d's real smile was so much prettier than that forced atrocity she'd worn every other time they'd met.

Moments later, in the cramped confines of the proprietor's office, she signed a contract for a year's work as the inn's head of security. She figured her probation with the Gardeners would take at least that long to sort out. And to her surprise, she no longer minded the wait.

The Priestess & The Trow

~ V ~

"Blessed be the goddess as she rests in your soul. Blessed be the goddess as she lives in your heart."

The Animation Chamber was a windowless room lit only by four standing candelabras. The flickering orange flames made shadows dance on the cracked adobe walls. Trina's sister priestesses surrounded her in a tightly packed circle, bare shoulder to bare shoulder, sarongs blending together in a continuous wall of shimmering amber. They extended their arms as they chanted and she felt their hands rest on flesh and silk, covering every part of her with pulsing heat.

"Blessed be the goddess as she wakes to new life. Blessed be the goddess as she dances within."

A hide drum beat out a slow, insistent rhythm.

TUM-da-da, TUM-da. TUM-da-da, TUM-da.

The hands moved to the beat, sliding over her body. A hot wet palm squeezed her shoulder. A pair of long nails slid down her spine. Delicate, small fingers cupped her breast. A smooth hand slid up her inner thigh.

Trina felt the tingling warmth of Demia the Dancing Goddess open and spread inside her like a flower. She tried to focus the energy as she'd been taught: letting the goddess' dance fill her awareness, guiding her every thought and movement. It was more difficult than it should have been. The harder she concentrated, the more her mind drifted to last night's excitement at the Dragonsbane.

"Blessed be the goddess as she raises you up. Blessed be the goddess as she flies to the sun."

Her sister priestesses pressed in close, smothering her in a group embrace. The air turned thick and hot as she sank into a pulsing ocean of perfumed flesh and contracting muscle, of breathy moans and sighs of, "Goddess be with you and in you," and, "Blessed be the dance."

Still, she couldn't stop thinking about Jeydah's fight. As much as she disliked the Trow Elf as a flatmate, there was something about the way she'd physically dominated those loutish stavemen that stirred something primal inside the barmaid.

She'd stared in amazement as the assassin fought six men twice her size. As much as she'd wanted to help, her feet had been rooted to the spot, not so much in fear as fascination. It was as though each of Jeydah's kicks and jabs was an ephemeral glimpse of something sacred: an image from one of her favorite dreams.

Shame all that beautiful power has to be wielded by such an intolerant vix, she thought, forcing her attention back to rite.

Guided by an unseen collective impulse, the crowd of priestesses pulled back from the group embrace. Trina joined them as they converged on another aspirant, raising prajja through chanting and touches, caresses and moans. There were forty-eight of them packed into the chamber so the ritual took most of the morning. By its end, everyone was breathless and soaked with sweat, heads spinning with dehydration and heightened sacral energy.

A chime sounded and all eyes turned to the Majjikphima Hilanda Pusmai. She cut an impressive figure, wearing a silk dress the deep red of Vadpa Kaengkaai wine, a long cloth of gold scarf wrapped around her neck and hips, and a matching band of actual gold adorned with emeralds on her smooth, high brow. Trina thought, however, that she would be impressive even without the regal attire, with her flawless bronze skin, sumptuous golden mane, and striking green eyes.

The Priestess & The Trow

"Sisters, you have been stirred to life," the high priestess intoned. "Your flames have quickened, your waters brought to froth, your spirits raised to abide in the heavens high o'er your unimportant flesh. You are now ready to enter the light."

And with that, the heavy double doors behind her glided outward on well-oiled hinges. Sunlight flooded the chamber, dazzling Trina's eyes as the press of bodies surged forward, carrying her along with them. Her head ached and her eyes flooded with tears, but she opened them wide anyway, unwilling to miss any part of the great courtyard in the Temple of the Cavorting Incarnate.

There were no castles in the Freelands, but if there were they would look like the Demian Temple. The white brick walls framed by tall palms enclosed a splendid profusion of rose bushes, bougainvillea, and greatflower trees, pruned to accent the flowing lines of the white marble fountains and benches. The marble and porcelain tiles felt warm on her bare feet as Trina and the other aspirants wended their way to the steps of the grand ballroom.

The building itself towered over them, its splendid façade held a gleaming brass gate with ornamental pillars on either side, carved in the likenesses of the Goddess Demia's handmaidens: minor goddesses embodying the virtues of sympathy and delight. Above the gate was a triangular entablature with a frieze depicting dancing spirits, divas, and other celestial beings and above that twin bell towers topped with golden domes each supporting the icon of the faith: a rod with twin serpents twisting around it, their bodies forming seven loops.

Majjikphima Hilanda watched over them as they approached, standing at the top of the stairway that spread like a mother's skirts out from the grand ballroom's entrance. The lower ranks of priestesses, adorned in orange and gold, stood like rows of marigolds on both sides of the red tiled steps. On plush seats to either side of the high priestess sat the honored donors and former students of the temple. There were Lars Baier, owner of the Lyonscall Theatrical Company, the fighter

Dana Duchess, and the siren, Kitana who'd been the first to talk to Trina about Demianism.

The high priestess had left the animation chamber and reached the top of the stairway very quickly, Trina realized, and without a trace of dishevelment or loss of breath. She wondered what mechanism the temple had used to accomplish such a feat, a niggling part of her mind worrying at the problem like a dog with a bone.

Before the steps lay a circular area with the aspirants forming two lines around its perimeter. In the center sat an altar, draped in a crimson cloth, holding four symbolic implements: a brass song horn, a copper mask, a silver chalice, and a golden key the size of Tina's forearm.

The chime sounded.

The majjikphima spread her arms and addressed them in a resounding tone.

"Who enters the garden of the goddess?"

As one they replied, "we who aspire to learn the dance."

"What dance is this?"

"The dance of life amongst the cords of fate, the dance of love upon the cords of consciousness, the dance of desire, and the dance that opens all doors."

"Come then and choose the instrument of your craft."

The first aspirant stepped forward from her place at the foot of the stairs, and approached altar. Trina recognized the girl from her classes and meditation sessions. Her name was… Ygrett? No, Irabilla: a pretty Terrellian girl who'd recently been signed as a dancer for The Angel Star Company.

She walked with a confident straight-backed sashay, her brilliant blonde hair swishing like a conductor's baton over her olive-skinned shoulders. Trina thought she would surely choose the mask, but she picked up the song horn instead, signifying her desire to take the Path of the Siren.

The device looked like a tulip made of brass. Easily held in one hand, it looked far too small to be an effective megaphone. It was, however, enchanted with finely etched runes and carefully positioned flecks of blue agate, cryolite, and other

The Priestess & The Trow

substances that vibrated at the same frequencies as people's voices. All these were activated by a blue dreamstone on its pommel that flickered with pale blue light that shone brighter the closer the aspirant held it to her throat.

"What, my child, is this?"

"The working instrument of a Siren."

"What is its value?"

"The instrument is worthless as is the one who bears it. Only the craft has value."

"Surrender then, and perform."

Next came the aspirant's ordeal. Irabilla took a deep breath, closing her eyes to better focus her prajja. The dreamstone flared in response, blazing the hot white of a miniature sun.

Then she sang, although the word "sang" hardly did the phenomenon justice. The spirit of the goddess flowed from her mouth in mesmerizing tendrils of sound, tugging and teasing the souls of all who listened. Her body swayed, her limbs twisted and swirled, their every movement designed to fascinate and arouse.

Majjikphima Hilanda and her retinue watched the performance dispassionately until its finish. When the singer concluded with a bow, everyone seated turned to the high priestess, who smiled and clapped her hands in polite applause. The rest followed suit, and the aspirant ascended the stairs to receive a garland of daisies and red hibiscus around her neck, commemorating her acceptance as a novice.

It wasn't until then that Trina realized the song had been a maudlin arrangement from the ballad of The Primrose and the Manticore. She'd never cared for the song before, thinking it too overplayed and melodramatic, but she'd found herself swept up in the singer's rendition nonetheless. Such was the nature of Demian wantcraft!

Several more aspirants stepped forward to proclaim their path, select the corresponding tool of their craft, and perform an ordeal. Most performances didn't go as smoothly as the first, two Sirens squeaking on high notes, a Changeling rolling

Adam Berk

her ankle during her dance, and an oral dissertation from one of the Matrons droning so monotonously that it put Trina in the deepest trance she'd experienced all day. There weren't any doorkeepers yet, but she knew there would be as a glance toward a partially overgrown garden path reveal three large, bare-chested men standing by a pile of silk blankets and cushions.

And then it was Trina's turn.

Here we go. She stepped forward, feeling the weight of a hundred pairs of eyes judging her every movement. *If this doesn't work, I can always choose the Path of the Changeling. At least I hope I can.*

Then she was standing at the altar looking down on the four tools of wantcraft. It would be so easy, she thought, to pick up that copper mask. She'd trained to take the Path of the Changeling: perfecting a soliloquy from *The Illusory Cuckold* as her ordeal. She knew she could deliver the performance perfectly; she should just do what she'd prepared to do and be done with it.

She reached out her hand, but instead of grasping the mask, she rested her fingers on the wine colored altar cloth in front of it. There was a flat, smooth shape under the fabric, just as Jeydah had said there would be. The discovery thrilled her more than she'd expected or even thought possible, and before she knew it she was pulling up the silk fabric and reaching under it with trembling hands.

Whispers hissed around her like wind, and murmurs rumbled like thunder as she pulled out the mirror.

"What in the abyss is that?" "Isn't that a tool for the Moon Path?" "Do we even *have* that anymore?"

It looked out of place next to the other tools with their ornate metalwork, runes and magic stones: a round, unframed sliver of glass fused with quicksilver and tin.

This is crazy, she thought. *I don't even know what the ordeal is for the Path of the Moon! What if I fail? What if the path requires something horrible, and that's why no one talks about it anymore? What if they ban me from the temple forever?*

The Priestess & The Trow

She looked at it as though the object could give her guidance somehow. All she saw was her own reflection—blue eyes wide and shadowed with consternation. But there was power in those eyes, she realized: a curious vitality unlike anything she'd seen in her sister aspirants.

And that was all the guidance she needed.

Holding the mirror in both hands, she turned and walked to the stairs. The figures seated at the top were a tableau of interest and perplexity. Dana Duchess sat on the edge of her seat, Kitana frowned with a pensive finger pressed to her lips. The Majjikphima, however, might as well have been carved from stone.

"What, my child, is this?"

"The working tool of a sister of the azure moon."

"What is its value?"

"The instrument is worthless as is the one who bears it. Only the craft has value."

"Right," said the high priestess. "That's enough of that, then."

She stood and clapped her hands gesturing for the three bare chested men to come forward. For a moment, Trina thought the Ordeal of the Moon was going to be like the Ordeal of the Doorkeeper, and she suddenly felt weak in the knees. But the men merely stood in a triangle around her as Majjikphima Hilanda ordered them to "Escort her to the tower."

The men guided her away from the circle, to the edge of the courtyard with light pulls and pushes on her back and shoulders. She didn't resist, but wondered if this was still part of the rite, or if she was being imprisoned for breaking a taboo. A furtive glance at high priestess and her retinue revealed naught but blank faces, and her fellow aspirants looked as confused as she was.

The tower, as it turned out, was a small, circular turret on the south wall of the courtyard. One of the men opened the door, and led her up a spiral staircase with the other two following close behind.

Adam Berk

The room at the top was by no means a prison cell: the two chairs had cushions, the sleeping pallet clean linens, the burnished maple floor was thoroughly swept. There was even a tall tri-fold mirror by a small table that could serve as a vanity if necessary.

"You're to wait here," said the man who'd led her up the stairs, "until the Majjikphima calls you."

"Calls me for what?"

"If *you* don't know, *I* sure don't," he replied with a sheepish shrug.

Despite the man's size, his looks had a boyish quality accentuated by his wide eyes, smooth cheeks, and hairless torso. He turned and left the chamber and Trina caught herself staring at his perfectly shaped posterior. What could such a well-crafted specimen of maleness possibly do for work, she wondered, when he wasn't assisting the Demian temple?

She heard faint click of the door at the foot of the stairwell locking.

That seems unnecessary, she thought.

The Demian temple always made a point of reminding its members they could leave any time they wanted. There were, after all, many competing spiritual groups in the Freelands, and imprisoning people against their will gave cults a bad name. That they were taking such measures now could only mean she'd given the powers that be a significant jolt.

"Approach then, Doorkeeper, and ready your thrice-locked portal!"

The high priestess' voice carried from the courtyard below, along with a low throbbing of drums. The room had four windows, but all but one of them were closed with heavy wooden shutters. Trina hurried to the open one, hoping it would afford her a view of the rite.

Figures, she thought, *that they'd wait 'til* now *to do a doorkeeper!*

The Ordeal of the Doorkeeper was the purest expression of wantcraft, raising ethereal geysers of prajja energy. Energy that other aspirants could potentially use in their own ordeals to improve their introductory rank. Gazing out the tower

The Priestess & The Trow

window, Trina found to her increasing consternation, that she had a clear view of the event but wouldn't be close enough to tap any of its energy.

"Let the key be tried!"

The aspiring doorkeeper held the instrument of her craft in her right hand while lowering herself onto a newly assembled pile of cushions with her left. The golden "key" was actually far too large to be used in any functional lock. Instead the pink and orange nodules of chudobaite and hummerite arrayed around its shaft were designed channel its bearer's desire into pulsating sonic vibrations. Trina heard a low hum followed by a collective gasp from the assembly as the aspirant put the key between her legs, sending a wave of prajja energy out to all in the vicinity.

"Let the first lock be breeched!"

The men who'd escorted Trina to the tower now approached the prostrate girl below, each body flawless, hairless, completely naked and fully aroused. Trina tried to focus, trying to summon her own energy with squeezes, rubs and caresses, opening her senses to any prajja that might drift her direction, but she felt nothing. It didn't help that the men's waddling swaggers kept reminding her of those arrogant stavemen back at the Dragonsbane: the way they'd ganged up on Jeydah when she was down, batons held at waist level, waggling in anticipation.

"Rreep?"

The barmaid cocked her head, bemused. Her thoughts about her flatmate had made a nearby birdcall sound just like Rhys, the Trow Elf's pet miffin. Then she looked down and gasped when she saw that very creature sitting on the windowsill looking up at her.

"Ho there, little guy. How in The Abyss did *you* get here?"

"I sent him."

Trina jumped as a voice rang in her head, as vivid and clear as the Majjikphima's in the rite below.

"Jeydah? What the pock is going on?"

"Let the second lock be breeched!"

Adam Berk

"Um, maybe you should bring Rhys inside, where you won't be distracted."

Trina glanced at the doorkeeper's ordeal. The aspirants in the circle all swayed and sighed in the ecstatic throes of prajja washing over them, but the only things the barmaid could perceive were distant grunts and slapping noises.

Gods, she thought. *Our rites look rather disgusting if you're not in the middle of them, don't they?*

Shaking her head in exasperation, she picked up the miffin and carried him into the chamber. She noticed Rhys had a collar with a little cloth bundle attached to it as the creature perched easily in her cradled arms. He was lighter than he looked, and she had to admit, his downy white feathers combined with his fluffy feline hindquarters made him very "squishy" indeed.

She set him on the table in front of the tri-fold mirror. There he sat glaring at her as she pulled a chair over and sat across from him.

"Well, well, well. Looks like the princess got herself locked in a tower and needs to be rescued. Surprise, surprise."

Trina's jaw dropped. Jeydah'd been the one to recommend the Moon Path in the first place. Did she really send her emissary just to give her a hard time?

"You can't be serious."

"Sorry, I couldn't resist. You really are in danger though. My contact at the temple finally got back to me this morning. Apparently there's a reason The Temple of the Cavorting Incarnate doesn't have any Moon Path oracles. They've always acted as checks to the Matron Path priestesses' power and Majjikphima Hilanda is leading a secret movement to eliminate them from the religion altogether."

"Wonderful."

Trina felt disgusted to her core. So that was it then? Was she to be barred from her true spiritual path because some power-hungry vix was staging a coup?

Pocking Angelwood! she thought. *Leave it to a polis of narcissists and egomaniacs to turn a beautiful spiritual craft into something ugly.*

"Let the third lock be breeched!"

The Priestess & The Trow

As if in answer to her thought, the rhythmic slapping sounds from outside rose to a feverish crescendo, culminating in a muffled shriek.

"So they're planning to what? Keep me here until the ritual's over, then have me excommunicated."

"No. Too many people saw you holding that mirror. If word got to the other temples that she'd denied an aspirant her ordeal, Hilanda's superiors would come down on her harder than Syndraxan zealots on a whoremonger."

"So..."

"They're going to give you an ordeal you can't possibly pass. Most likely a battle of rupahms with the Majjikphima herself."

"But that's ridiculous!" Trina exclaimed. "I won't stand a chance. Nobody would!"

Even if she could channel the song of the goddess as she had in Shosev's fairy grove, her uncle had been taken by surprise. The high priestess was expecting such an attack, and had been communing with the goddess for many years longer than she.

"That's the idea, dolly! The most sensible thing to do right now is to run. Get as far away from the temple as you can and hope the high priestess is okay with a former aspirant knowing her bosky plans—at least enough not to send someone like me after you."

Trina's mind raced. The suspended assassin was right, of course. There was no way Mistress Hilanda would allow her to walk freely about the polis knowing what she knew about the temple's secrets.

She'd have to leave immediately, throwing Garret, her job, and the good stable life she'd made for herself right in the shest bucket! And she certainly couldn't risk contacting any temples to further her spiritual education. The thought made her breathless with rage.

"And what if I don't *want* to run away?" she whispered.

Jeydah's voice laughed in her head.

"I thought you might say that. We don't see eye to eye on much, but at least we both have zero tolerance for trollshest. Look in the pouch on Rhys' collar."

Adam Berk

Trina did as she was bade. The miffin, thinking she was reaching out to pet him began to flop about on the table like a newly caught fish, and the barmaid nearly wrenched a finger out of its socket trying to remove the collar.

The pouch, she noticed, was a small black sequestery sack—the kind the Lascivian mages used to hold their charged stones and herbs. Inside she found cashew nuts mixed with dried red flower petals. It wasn't until she dumped the contents into her hand that she felt the telltale tingle of ensorcelled substance.

"Lumen nuts?"

"Yes. With a saffron pairing to raise your prajja. Try to keep a cool head when you take them; the charger I bought 'em from nearly killed himself making them. And don't get addicted!"

Trina didn't need to be told that. She stared at the nuts as though they'd been picked out of a pile of fresh cockatrice droppings. She knew how addictive the little moon-shaped stimulants could be. She'd once dated a playwright who'd stolen a month's rent from her to feed his habit. If this was truly the only way…

A latch clicked and the door at the bottom of the tower's stairwell opened. Trina popped the nuts and saffron in her mouth, chewed and swallowed without a second thought. She then grabbed Rhys, who was busy gouging tiny holes in the tabletop with his beak, and chucked the miffin out the window. He squawked in surprise, flapping his wings frantically, before swooping in a circle to glare at her, and flying off, tail twitching in annoyance.

"Aspirant UiConnal, are you prepared?"

Trina turned to find the same bare-chested man who'd locked her in the tower several drams earlier. Only this time, his hair was disheveled, his skin slick with sweat and his boyish eyes sparkling with a light only a newly wetted wand could bestow.

"As much as I'll ever be."

She walked by the man to the stairway, breathing in as she passed, the rich salty musk pervading his body. On impulse,

The Priestess & The Trow

she reached out brushing her fingertips across his thick, wet shoulder. And to her surprise, prajja energy flowed from him into her as easily as ale from a tankard.

As she stepped out the tower door into the bright afternoon sun, she realized she could feel prajja everywhere. Every bird and squirrel, every flower and tree sang and danced around her, much as it had in her uncle's fairy grove. But it was different this time: more frantic as though each living thing were cognizant of its own mortality and wanted to screw every other living thing as much as possible before their deaths.

Also, she didn't remember the Dance of the Goddess feeling this... good! She felt as though she were floating as she approached the circle of aspirants still standing before the terra cotta steps. The air grew warmer, the sunlight brighter, until every fear and doubt withered and vanished.

There's no way I can lose, she thought, as she felt oceans of prajja energy crashing through her. *I'm rotpocking invincible!*

Every part of her shone like the sun. Every part of her vibrated to a perfect G sharp major chord. She was light incarnate. By the abyss, she pocking *was* the Goddess!

"Well child," Majjikphima Hilanda intoned (Trina jumped as she realized she was already standing before the steps). "You wish to take the Path of the Moon, is that it? Without even knowing what that entails?"

"G'on Great Mother!" the barmaid blurted out. "It obviously entails exploring the unknown, dunnit? Why else'd all you bosky vixes keep it secret? So *I'd* have to take the initiative and explore it *myself!*"

Yes! That was amazing! I'm so pocking brilliant right now!

"Well then," said the high priestess. "You certainly have an impressive level of dedication. Your kundha is simple. Convince me to kiss you, and you can stay."

The Majjikphima descended the stairway, long golden hair and cloth of gold scarf flaring behind her in the warm dry breeze. From the tilt of her head, to the positioning of her sandaled feet, her every step was a deliberate and beautiful act of dominance. When she at last stood across from Trina in the midst of the circle, the barmaid felt the woman's charisma as a palpable force, penetrating to the very depths of her being.

It's beginning already, she realized. *The dance of charisma with desire.*

"Mistress Hilanda," she said, her body flowing into the beguiling postures of her rupahms, "Surely you don't see me as a threat to your supremacy. All I do comes from one place. My devotion to your teachings. My love for you."

The rupahms came easier to her than they ever had, *let's-steal-treasure-together* turning to *I'm-your-lovelorn-slave* at the perfect point to snare Hilanda's core chadaka. In her mind's eye, Trina saw a golden cord of astral light unwinding from the high priestess' solar plexus. She snared it and pulled it around her, the sensation as vivid as putting on a shawl.

"Sweet child," the Majjikphima responded, her voice suddenly breathless as she reeled from her aspirant's sudden burst of power. "You are mistaken. Your dance comes not from love of me, or even love of Demia's craft. It comes from selfishness, pride, and need to dominate."

Hilanda's rupahms were flawless. *Ailing-mother's-sighs* fell into *your-knife-slowly-pierces-my-flesh,* which opened into a heart-wrenching series of movements Trina had never even seen before. Only the aspirant's lumen nut-heightened senses enabled her to retract her heart chadaka's cord before the high priestess could snare it.

"Mother! How can you call me selfish? You yourself know power must be seized at the opportune moment. I empower myself to serve the goddess, just like you. I yearn above all else to unify Ardyn in love, just like you. Because I love you. Because I *am* you."

Captive-maiden's-cry swelled into *offerings-to-my-goddess,* which blossomed into *you-found-my-secret-treat-now-share-it-with-me.* She closed the distance between the high priestess and herself, her every expression and movement hauling on Hilanda's core chadaka's cord like a dockworker on a tow cable.

It was a primitive strategy, but the only one available. The majjikphima kept all her other chadakas close to her center.

The Priestess & The Trow

Still, it was working! The high priestess came within arm's length, and Trina parted her lips to receive her kiss.

"Sweetling," she said, touching the aspirant's cheek with her perfect porcelain fingers. "You are not me. How can you be, little fool, when I've never used narcotics to enhance my craft."

She spun about then, the ends of her hair whisking past Trina's reaching lips, and executed a flawless combination of *dropping-my-soiled-cloak*, *stepping-on-a-dying-basilisk,* and *walking-with-a-dragon-at-my-back*. The aspirant gasped as the majjikphima's cords lashed out striking her chadakas in rapid succession. It felt as though her soul were being buffeted by high winds.

"You should purge them right now."

Trina dropped to her knees and wretched before she even knew what hit her. Her mind raced as she struggled to counter Hilanda's command, but it had already taken affect. A torrent of hot bilious fluid rushed into her mouth, and onto the porcelain tile, taking with it the effects of the lumen nuts and enchanted saffron.

"Look at you," said the high priestess, drawing herself up into *tower-above-all-enemies*. "Strutting about like you know something, while you profane our sacred craft with drugs. What shame you must feel!"

And Trina did feel shame. It was dark and heavy. It pressed her down—a serving tray piled with a thousand mismade orders. Even knowing the sensation was all conjured by Mistress Hilanda's wantcraft couldn't keep her from sliding into utter despair.

What a fool she was! Followers of the Moon Path were supposed to be wise as the Mystican Mystics. She was naught but a rotpocking barmaid and always would be.

Her vision darkened. Someone put a handle in front of her and she grabbed it reflexively, as though she were drowning, and it was the only thing floating on her churning waves of angst. Looking down, she realized what it was: a thin-bladed dagger. The hilt, being gold and mother of pearl, looked a perfect fit for the Demian temple's rite, but the blade's edge was visibly sharp, and it's needle-sharp point was far from ceremonial.

"You should take your life."

The idea was a jasmine scented candle lit in the foul dark bog of her mind. She could do it! She could end all life's pains and disappointments with one quick thrust.

The blade was so thin and sharp it positively begged to slide between her ribs. Her aching heart yearned for its kiss. At some point, she realized, she'd pushed down the top of her sarong exposing the flesh just above her left breast. The dagger's tip was hard and cold against her skin.

"Think, child, of how good it will feel—"

It would be so easy. One quick thrust. Why didn't she just end it already?

Because, she realized, she'd been here before.

She'd been sixteen when she'd run away from her Uncle Shosev's manor, and all the vile things he'd done to her. With nothing but her wits and the clothes on her back, the following years had been a chaotic cavalcade of running, begging and stealing for survival. She'd spent some moons homeless and begging, others shacked up with musicians, entertainers or what-have-you, others eating gruel and sleeping on straw at an Ardainite convent. The days all blurred to a kaleidoscopic hodgepodge in her head, but the nights were vivid and never to be forgotten.

"—to release the rotting failure of your life once and for all—"

Some nights she'd curl on hard stone after a day of not eating. Some nights she'd spent tangled in strange-smelling sheets with a man she'd met only hours before. And most nights—nearly every gods-damned one—she'd lain awake thinking of all the terrible things she'd done, hating herself, and thinking of all the ways she could end her horrible rotpocked life.

But she'd always beaten it, she realized, as a hot drop of blood bloomed under the dagger's point and rolled down between her breasts. She'd gotten up the next day, put on the

The Priestess & The Trow

smiles and charms she'd worn as armor, and sallied forth into Angelwood's torrid streets to live another day.

"—into oblivion."

Only one way to beat back the bleakness, Trina thought. *Got to get out of myself.*

She raised her head and cast about looking for something she could use: some handhold to grasp as the black torrents of hateful memories assaulted her mind. She looked to her fellow aspirants, but they refused to meet her gaze—too disgusted with her failure, or fearful of their own to get involved. She looked to the majjikphima's guests still seated at the top of the stairs. Lars Baier was distracted with a pretty young priestess on his lap, giggling and squirming as his knobby old hands crawled like stick insects over her sarong. He didn't even notice Trina's ordeal much less care. Dana Duchess shot her an encouraging look, but that was all.

But then she saw the siren Kitana, and it was as though she'd lit a candle in a hall of mirrors. Something about Trina's ordeal had struck a sympathetic chord in the singer. The aspirant looked into the woman's perfect green eyes.

They shone with tears.

Seizing her opportunity, Trina turned her pathetic expression and prostrate posture into *lovelorn-slave's-surrender* and linked Kitana's heart chadaka with her own.

> *My hero and beloved one,*
> *Morn me not when my life's gone.*
> *The Fae wood has heard our true-spoken words*
> *The trees ring with our song.*

Though Trina had never had much faith in her singing ability, the words sprang from her lips nonetheless. Her voice was timorous, weak, and had scant resemblance to the transcendent tones of a Siren's song, yet Kitana reacted to it nonetheless. Rising to her feet as though pulled by the music itself, the singer joined in the duet.

Adam Berk

Seasons turn, though our love always burns
It may be hid 'neath frost and snow.
You must be brave and faithful;
It will warm and grow!

So entranced was Trina by the experience of singing a duet with the legendary Siren, she didn't even remember where she knew the song from. When she did, the sudden urge to throw back her head and laugh like a lunatic nearly broke the spell. It was the final duet of *The Primrose and the Manticore*, when Hans the Knight of the Manticore Order loses Primrose, his beloved fairy bride to plague, and was, in Trina's opinion, the most maudlin thing ever written.

Guess even dreffy popular music has its uses, she thought.

Clergy and guests alike watched enthralled as the aspirant and the siren sang to each other as knight and fairy princess. Majjikphima Hilanda looked back and forth between them, a growing tension around her eyes the only indicator of her consternation. Then, when it occurred to her what Trina might do with her siren thrall, she rushed to action: addressing, commanding, and cajoling each of them in turn to cease their silly digression at once, and "give the rite the gravity it deserved."

But Kitana was fully absorbed in her music, and Trina knew this was the only chance of beating the High Priestess and surviving her ordeal.

Oh my love, my knight and champion,
I can feel your burning ire.
You must let me go, or the seeds that we sewed
Will perish in the fire.

Trina performed Princess Primrose's final lyrics, acting out her death as only a wantcrafter on the Changeling Path could act, and Kitana responded, throwing herself into Hans' angst-driven throes. As the aspirant fell to the ground, "dying" however, she ad-libbed a final command to the ensorcelled

The Priestess & The Trow

Siren.

"Sing to your utmost power, my love. Sing 'til it burns them all to ash!"

"No!"

The Majjikphima called out, but Kitana's song had already begun. Trina used the dagger in her hands to cut two chunks of fabric from her sarong and stuff them in her ears. Even muffled, the Siren's song was heart-wrenching as she cried out the sorrow and rage of Hans the Manticore Knight with sounds so inhuman, so beautiful, so terrible, that the aspirant felt flayed to her very soul.

The rest of the crowd, however, took the full brunt of the Siren's Frenzy Song. They crumpled like grass blades in a brushfire, wailing and tearing at their clothing and flesh.

Even Hilanda's special guests at the top of the stairway were affected. Dana Duchess cried on her hands and knees, driving her head over and over again into the polished marble. Lars Baier and pretty young priestess rolled about on the stairs gnawing each other bloody like rabid wolves.

"Make her stop it!" Hilanda cried.

She was on her knees, all composure forgotten, rivers of tears streaking her perfect cheekbones. The effect would have been satisfying, if Trina hadn't fallen to the ground herself as even the wadded silk filtered tones of the Kitana's song seemed to jam-pack every emotion she'd ever felt into her head and chest.

"I will," the aspirant shouted above the abyssal wails around her, "when you kiss me, you great evil vix!"

A look of blind animal rage flashed across the priestess' face, then was suppressed as the woman forced her features into composure so serene it was terrible to behold. Suddenly, Trina feared the high priestess would sacrifice them all in her obstinance. Instead, the high priestess grabbed the back of the aspirant's head and pressed her mouth to hers as though trying to leave a mark.

Trina tensed in shock, then embraced the Majjikphima with gusto as she savored her victory along with the taste of cinnamon and vanilla on woman's pudding-soft lips. She reeled after they parted, but rose and commanded Kitana to be silent. She then severed her psychic bond with the Siren.

The singer shuddered in response: chest heaving, mouth agape in an incredulous grin, green eyes wide and darting every which way as though trying to deduce whether she should be appalled or elated by the devastation wrought by her talents. The aspirants and priestesses who'd been caught in the throes of the frenzy song helped each other to their feet. The courtyard filled with elated laughter and tittering as though they'd all gotten off the Wizard's Wheel at the Pinnacle and not just escaped from the brink of death.

"You have power, child," Hilanda hissed in Trina's ear, "and I have to respect that. But don't think that being on the Moon Path entitles you to get in my way. If I hear even a hint of a rumor about any insubordination or—"

"I'm leaving, Great Mother," said Trina. "As soon as I'm done with my year as a novice, Garret and I are moving to Frank."

She knew it was the right move as she felt the tension easing out of the woman behind her. Still, Garret and she had only given moving away together the most cursory of conversations. She prayed to Demia and every other deity she knew that her burly paramour would understand.

"Yes."

The Majjikphima's hands rested on her shoulders like the talons of a sleeping eagle: a light touch that carried dark promises.

"I think that would be for the best. If you excel in your studies, as you have in your ordeal, I'll put in a commendation for you at the Temple of the Luminous Loops."

The high priestess gave her shoulders a lingering squeeze, then ascended the stairway. On reaching the top, she spread her arms and proclaimed in a voice ringing sweet and true as the temple bells that for the first time in years the Temple of the Cavorting Incarnate had a new initiate of the Path of the Moon. She then gave a stirring speech about how because this

The Priestess & The Trow

spiritual road was so sacred, she'd needed to test the aspirant with extreme measures, and assured them that neither Trina nor any of the spectators were ever in danger.

Trina, of course, knew differently. She watched the Majjikphima's movements as she spoke, recognizing *giving-out-holiday-sweets* and *mother-bringing-the-nightlamp*. She couldn't see anyone's chadakas but could tell by the crowd's adoring smiles and cheers that the charismatic high priestess had caught them all.

Gods and spirits, thought the newly raised novice, *do I have to make enemies everywhere I go?*

The Majjikphima and her officiators resumed the ritual, with several girls left to take the paths of Siren, Changeling, Matron and Doorkeeper, until the sky turned orange in the west and the sun dipped below the courtyard wall. At the close of the rite, the sacred paraphernalia were cleared and tables of sumptuous food and drink were arranged in their place. Musicians appeared and played their instruments on daises and enclaves scattered throughout the courtyard.

Trina noticed Farian Daringsford strumming his lute beneath a mulberry tree while a crowd of novices stared at him with sparkling eyes. Their eyes met, he winked and she couldn't stop herself from laughing. From what she'd seen, the barkeep bard had his own brand of wantcraft. She'd have to watch that one—but not too closely.

Feeling more exhausted than exuberant, Trina grabbed a trencher full of roast sweetbeans, pushed past the crowds as they poured through the temple's main entrance, and haled a harkey cab on Goddess Boulevard. After all she'd been through, she needed the serenity of her own chair in her own flat, reading one of her own books—preferably about something besides wantcraft for a change! Besides, there was someone there that she very much wanted to talk to.

Adam Berk

~ VI ~

"You could always quit, you know."

Jeydah placed the teapot in the middle of the table and handed Trina her cup. She'd finished listening to the newly raised novice's account of her perilous ordeal, concluding with the Majjikphima's not-too-subtle threats on her life. The Trow Elf had kept uncharacteristically quiet through the tale, determined to see Trina's religion as a means of empowerment as opposed to the megalomaniac campaign of libidinous conquest the assassin had always thought it to be.

"Right, quit," Trina scoffed, turning her empty teacup over and over in her hands. "And do what? Spend the rest of my life charming rich pockers into buying more expensive bottles of wine? I felt the presence of the Dancing Goddess, for gods' sake! I don't know what her plans for me are, but I'd like to think they're a bit more impressive than that."

Jeydah nodded as she measured several spoonfuls of honey into her empty cup.

"True, Demia certainly seems to be doing well by you so far. If leading you into and out of one dangerous situation after another is what you're after, that is."

Trina leaned back in her seat with a flustered groan.

"That's how I know I'm on the right path. Nothing that mean's anything's ever just given to you. If I spent my life

The Priestess & The Trow

taking the easy way, I'd be back in Alsyra warming the bed of some lecherous old lord."

"As opposed to committing to a year of servitude and sex with strangers as a novice while you wait on kullbung guests at the Dragonsbane and flob about with a man old enough to be your father."

The barmaid flushed and puffed up as she tried to concoct a hasty retort.

"But it's alright," the elf quickly added, pouring a little hot water in her cup and swirling it as she waited for the tealeaves to steep. "Because all of it's your choice. And that's what makes the difference."

The thought gave the assassin pause. It occurred to her how refreshing it had been to take the job as the Dragonsbane Inn's chief of security on her own terms instead of being assigned to it by the Gardeners. Perhaps following one's heart *was* the most important thing.

"Of course," she contemplated aloud, "you won't get much choice at all if Majjikphima Hilanda sees you as a threat again."

"Pock her!" Trina snarled.

She grabbed the pot and poured Jeydah the first cup.

"I decided a long time ago that there's only one person who gets a say in what I do with my life!"

Jeydah had to chuckle at that. It sounded so much like something she would have said in her younger years. Oak and iron! She'd said it the other day now that she thought of it!

"You know, princess, you and I might have more in common than I'd like to admit."

"Is that why we annoy the shest out of each other?"

"Ha! You think? That and you're apparently incapable of cleaning a plate after you use it."

"I told you, I was running late to work! Gods forbid anything in this flat should be less than spotless for more than a dram…"

They talked long into the night, exchanging snips and barbs like coins in a card game. Jeydah enjoyed the exchange.

Adam Berk

Her life as an assassin had kept her from having any close friendships for years, and while her arrangement with Trina wasn't that, it had enough of its features to fill the role.

And for the moment, she couldn't imagine anything more satisfying.

The Priestess & The Trow

Author's Note

Hail, travellers! Thank you for taking another journey with me to the Freelands of Ardyn for a stay at The Dragonsbane Inn.

Be sure to follow @AdamBerkWriter on Instagram and Twitter for updates, new world-building developments and, of course, that grand announcement in the not too distant future when a sign with a major publisher! That handle will also work for my Patreon account if you're feeling generous. You can also buy more books or join my mailing list at AdamBerkWriter.com

Another way you can help is to leave a brief review on Amazon, Goodreads, your local paper, the walls of bathroom stalls, etc. For those of you who know where I work: show me a review and I'll buy you a drink. Depending on my mood, using Freelandish slang while you give me your order might yield a similar result.

Thanks again,

Your writer and barkeep,

Adam Berk

Appendix

A Guide to Freelandish Slang

And Other Terms

Abis - Same as Abyss, but pronounced AH-bis. The Freelandish word for hell. Portmanteau word combining the Trophican "Abyss" with the Syndraxan *Ajasi* (pron. AH-ja-see).

Abyss – aka the Great Abyss. Place of punishment for evil souls upon their death according to Trophican Ardainite and Evanescicle religions.

Adder – also *Addah*. The male organ as great, large or massive. From the Gimadran word Adpha, meaning great, greatness or phallus.

Ardanite – One of the most popular religions on Ardyn. Views the legendary hero Ardath Dragonsbane as an "avatar of light" and his slaying of the dragon Syngyde, and sundering of The Paragon of Darkness as an act of universal cleansing and salvation.

Brahda – A term of endearment. Same usage as "brother", although for a friend instead of a literal relative. From the Gimadran *brao dong* meaning family friend.

Bosflob – A con job, particularly one of a light-hearted nature. Portmanteau of "bosky" and "flob".

Adam Berk

Bosky - Shady, nefarious. From the Old Trophican word for wooded.

Byss-pit - A "hell-hole", or an unpleasant place to work, reside, etc. From the words Abyss and pit.

Byss-blighted – Same usage as goddamned. rel. byss-blasted, byss-buggered, or byss-pocked.

Blackrobe – Term of contempt for an entertainments business professional, referencing the black robes commonly worn by Lascivian Mages. E.g. "I wanted a spectacular battle scene in my play, but the pocking *blackrobes* said we didn't have the budget for it."

Blatherrach – Literally, one who assaults others with blather. A person given to voluble, empty talk.

Bucket - Common word for chamber pot, i.e. "in the bucket" which is to say, "down the drain".

Buckethead – One who, metaphorically speaking, has a chamber pot where his brains should be.

Bung - Same usage as "asshole", more commonly in reference to the anatomical part than the type of person (who would more commonly be called a "kullbung").

Cestodal Grafting Imbuement (CGI) – Magecraft term for the process of infesting a performer with magically enhanced tine worms to make the subject heal faster and able to attach severed appendages.

Collywallies - Feelings of nervous apprehension. From "colic" and the Trophican term, collywobbles.

Collywald - A coward. One who is prone to "getting the collywallies".

The Priestess & The Trow

Chucking Buckets - Term for one who is violently enraged. Originated with the famously insane Angelwood Polis Councilman John Hedwig, who after being cheated by a whore in a hotel suite, began throwing chamber pots about the place in a fit of rage.

Chirk - to cheer (usually followed by "up"). Also, a shrill, chirping noise.

Chirkyjerk - An annoyingly cheerful person.

Chop - to banter, usually in an argumentative way, i.e. "just choppin' ya 'bout."

Clopper - Racial slur for centaur. More commonly used in the Mystican Countries, especially Medan.

Cockalorum - a self-important little man.

Cup – Fifty drams, two thousand five hundred drops, or 0.694 of an hour. There are 36 cups in a day, which is divided into quarters of nine. i.e. "three cups past dawn" is about 8 in the morning, and "eight cups past noon" is around 6 in the evening.

Cudgot – Originally "cut jot" or ¼ of the copper coin that is the smallest denomination of Freelandish currency.

Cutmark – Silver coin equal to ¼ of a mark. Refers to the seventy-five-year period after The Moonflower Purchases when silver marks were literally cut into quarters.

Danglestalk – Literally a man who is impotent. Metaphorically a man who is dull, boring, and/or lacking sex-drive.

Dapper - a waiter, or male servant. Aberration of dapifer.

Devandracal – A fundamentalist sect of the Ardanite religion that views the death of the dragon Syngyde at the hand of Ardath Dragonsbane as the conquest of all good over the conquest of all evil. Their adherents believe it necessary to continually slay their "personal dragons" in a lifestyle of purity and abstention.

Dim Dolly – Ditz or bimbo. A scatterbrained woman.

Dolly - A casual term of endearment, used mostly in the Angelwood entertainment industries. Similar usage to "Babe" or "Sweetie". Variants include, dollywally, dollykins, dollywallykins, etc. From the Gimadran word *doulchika* meaning sweet little girl.

Dram – as a measurement of time, 50 drops or approximately a minute. Originates with the Freelands' use of waterclocks.

Drop – as a measurement of time, about a second. i.e. "Hold a drop!" meaning "Wait a second."

Dref - schlock. Corny or overused subject matter as from a song or play. From the Gimadran word, *drepha* meaning "happy" as used in *pryohka drepha*, a slapstick comedy play. rel. "dreffy"

Fenmark – Highest denomination of Freelandish currency, a gold coin equal in value to 100 silver marks.

Flob - To talk or stand idly with no particular purpose. i.e. to "flob about" means to "hang out."

Frepp - An awkward, useless person. From the Gimadran *phrepongo*, a criminal who keeps getting caught.

Freppish - Similar usage to "wussy", but with more of a furtive, nervous, and possibly guilty connotation.

Fuzzberries – Testicles. Also, an actual variety of berry covered with an inedible light purple, fuzzy rind. The taste is

The Priestess & The Trow

like a lychee berry crossed with a kiwifruit.

Gimmie – Offensive pejorative for Gimadran.

Gong – crazy in a good way, usually in reference to a particularly fun party or other thrilling event. From the Gimadran *gahti* meaning backwards or insane.

Gonnyrot – The infamous sexually transmitted pox that plagued the early Mystican settlers of the Freelands. The name "Gonny" is a derisive term for Yllgoni people, particularly the sailors from Yllgon who were thought to be the origin of the virus.

Greenie – Offensive pejorative for goblin.

Guv – A term of respect, although often used ironically on outsiders by the Freelands' criminal elements.

Guvny – Prudish. From the word governor, the highest state office in the Freelands.

Harkey – a.k.a. Harkey Coach or Harkey Cart. Preferred means of public transportation in Angelwood and many other Freelandish poleis. Horse drawn carriages with wide seats named for the Harceigh Region of Corwbha which supplied early Freelandish settlers with horses. The horses' harnesses are thaumacrafted so the beasts can run faster and longer without tiring.

Harkey Horse – A common metaphoric standard for speed or hard work, i.e. "swift as a harkey horse" or "working hard as a harkey horse".

Hawmark – A silver coin worth ½ a mark. From the period seventy-five years after The Moonflower Purchases when silver marks were literally cut in half.

Hodgot – A copper coin worth ½ of a jot.

Adam Berk

Hedwig – i.e. "going hedwig". Angry to the point of insanity. Refers to a famous Angelwood councilman named Hedwig who was known to fly into fits of rage (see chucking buckets).

Holli – Exciting or stimulating. Commonly used in reference to attractive women. From the Gimadran *Chahoni* or feminine principle.

Honi – Vagina; same usage as "pussy". Pronounced HOH-nee. From the Gimadran *Chahoni* or feminine principle. Commonly punned with the Mystican common word "honey" in colloquialisms, i.e. "He put his dipper in her honeypot."

Jawdy – Sleazy. From the Gimadra *Mahkjohdhi* meaning the same.

Kannie-boy – offensive slur for a gay or effeminate man.

Kaoflob – To trash talk someone else's performance of a task you are incapable of doing. From the Gimadran *tikao* meaning "manure" and the slang term *flob* meaning to talk idly or "hang out".

Kapistarosolam – "Land of mindless indulgence". Derisive Syndraxan colloquialism for the Empire of Gimadra

Koudga – Unfortunate fellow or chap (usually, but not always, male). From the Gimadran *tikaojana* meaning "a slave who shovels manure".

Koke – Same usage as "cool". From the Gimadran *Kahokeh* meaning "rod of authority" - their divine masculine principal.

Kokachoni - Copacetic, having pleasant, mellow vibes. From the Gimadran *Kahokeh i'Chahoni* - their divine balance of masculine and feminine energies. *Chahoni* means "cavern of spirits".

Krashi – A female man-eating demon from Gimadran

The Priestess & The Trow

folklore. Also, a term of contempt for any unpleasant woman.

Kull – Same usage as "ass", usually in reference to the anatomical part, not the type of person. From the Gimadran word *kouli* meaning butt.

Kullbung – Same usage as "asshole", more commonly in reference to the type of person, rather than the anatomical part.

Kulljot – A sexual partner valued for looks over substance or, in a more literal sense, one's "piece of ass".

Mark – A silver coin that's the standard measure of Freelandish currency.

Mog – Head. Possibly of ancient Medanite origins; same root meaning of the name "Mogu", who is the god of performers, thieves, and basically anyone who has to think on his/her feet.

Mog-blotted – muddle-headed, as from regular consumption of alcohol.

Mollyboy – a gay or effeminate man.

Muddlemog – a ditzy, careless person. One who obsesses over useless things.

Noddies – testicles. From the Mystican Common word nodule meaning small knot or knob.

Palabhandi – "Backwards land": the derisive Gimadran colloquialism for the Syndraxan Empire.

Palacka – adj. stupid; mentally deficient, or n. one who is lacking in basic mental functions. From the Gimadran *palah gahti* meaning backward-moving.

Palagong – slow, apathetic, backwards thinking or moving.

Adam Berk

Paragite – balls of paper reeds or other soft grasses wrapped around party favors and hung from the ceiling for the Sunderfest holiday.

Paragon of Darkness – Mythical object Ardath Dragonsbane was said to have sundered while fighting the dragon Syngyde. Although no one knows what it looked like or if it existed at all, it is most commonly depicted as a smooth black sphere.

Pish – To ruin, dismiss, or make valueless. From the Gimadran *pishwa* meaning rubbish.

Pish ya pisser – To destroy one's credibility or reputation.

Pock – To use sexually. Also used as a generic vulgarity, i.e. "Get that pocking carriage out of the way!" or "The staveman caught me stealing, so now I'm pocked!" Originated with the rampant sexually transmitted diseases when the Freelands were first being colonized.

Pockstocker - a whoremonger or pimp.

Pongo – A Gimadran term of endearment meaning "big, dumb, and lovable person". From the Gimadran word *phrepongo* meaning a criminal who always gets caught.

Poofy - An effeminate man. Unknown origin.

Prassy – Behaving with the fussiness of a spoiled princess. Unknown origin.

Rach - Pronounced "rawch". To beat. From the Gimedran *warachee*, which is a type of sandal often used by Gimadran peasant women to beat unruly children.

Ray – The current arrangement, plan or circumstance, i.e. "What's the ray with that roast cockatrice? Are you saving it for company, or can anyone dig in?" From the term "array" used by Lascivian Mages to describe different placements of

The Priestess & The Trow

materiae in their enchantments.

Req – From "requite". A food and hospitality term: to wave payment of a meal, purchase, or service in compensation for the unsatisfactory quality thereof.

Rock-mogged – Stupid. Having a head like a rock.

Sandie – Offensive pejorative for Syndraxan.

Shest – Vulgar term for fecal excrement i.e. "trollshest".

Shest Bucket – A chamber pot.

Shestmog – One with disgusting values. One who has a head full of shest.

Shest Shover – Offensive term for a gay man.

Siren – A singer magically enhanced with visual and vocal effects, trained by the Demian Temple of the Cavorting Incarnate to entrance audiences with her voice and movements.

Snarf – To caress with tongue and mouth.

Sneck – A kiss or to kiss.

Snollygoster – A clever, unscrupulous person.

Snollygeck - To kiss with tongue and groping. To take advantage of sexually.

Snollyhole – One's mouth, especially if one is a snollygoster.

Sod Rod – An iron baton used by Lascivian Mages for grounding energy and by gang members for knocking people unconscious

Sparge – Ejaculate or the act of ejaculating

Adam Berk

Specky – Amazing to behold. From the Mystican Common word *spectacular*.

Stalk – The male member, especially when erect, a.k.a. pockstalk

Stalkpocker – Someone (usually a man) who has promiscuous sex with (other) men.

Stalk-steered – The condition of being driven primarily by one's desire for sex. syn. wand-willed

Teedee – "Very". From the Gimadran, *atido*.

Thaumacraft – a system of magic used by Lascivian Mages that crafts and utilizes magical tools.

Thaumafect – An object enchanted with runic script and charged materials for a specific purpose. A charm.

Twinklies – Eyes, especially those of a pretty girl (i.e. twinklie blues)

Vacky – Shallow. Having no intellectual depth.

Vix – A beautiful woman whose beauty endows her with an inflated sense of entitlement. Same usage as "bitch" but with more positive connotation.

Wig off – To upset to the point of violence. Ref. Councilman Hedwig, see above.

ABOUT THE AUTHOR

In the early 2000s Adam Berk went to college in Los Angeles to study film, and stayed there to try to be a movie star. After growing disgusted with the entertainment industry (and his many unsuccessful attempts to be a part of it), he got a Master's of Professional Writing degree from the University of Southern California and left town. He now lives in Salem Massachusetts where he tends bar, studies the occult with his witchy wife, and writes silly stories about magic and mythic beasts. He has never been happier.

Made in United States
North Haven, CT
11 April 2023